Cum For Me *Volume 4*
So Horny

Ca$h & Company

Lock Down Publications & Ca$h Whispers
Cum For Me 4
A Collection of Erotic Tales

Ca$h & Company

Lock Down Publications
P.O. Box 870494
Mesquite, Tx 75187

Visit our website at **www.lockdownpublications.com**

Copyright 2018 Cum For Me 4

First Edition December 2018
Printed in the United States of America
This is a work of fiction. Names, characters, places, and incidents either are products of the author's imagination or are used fictitiously. Any similarity to actual events or locales or persons, living or dead, is entirely coincidental.
Cover design and layout by: Dynasty's Cover Me
Book interior design by: Shawn Walker
Edited by: Lashonda Johnson

Stay Connected with Us!

Text **LOCKDOWN** to 22828 to stay up-to-date with new releases, sneak peaks, contests and more...

Thank you!

Submission Guideline.

Submit the first three chapters of your completed manuscript to <u>ldpsubmissions@gmail.com</u>, subject line: Your book's title. The manuscript must be in a .doc file and sent as an attachment. Document should be in Times New Roman, double spaced and in size 12 font. Also, provide your synopsis and full contact information. If sending multiple submissions, they must each be in a separate email.

Have a story but no way to send it electronically? You can still submit to LDP/Ca$h Presents. Send in the first three chapters, written or typed, of your completed manuscript to:

LDP: Submissions Dept
Po Box 870494
Mesquite, Tx 75187

DO NOT send original manuscript. Must be a duplicate.

Provide your synopsis and a cover letter containing your full contact information.

Thanks for considering LDP and Ca$h Presents.

These stories are brought to you by T.J. Edwards.
Enjoy them!

Ca$h & Company

Caught Slipping

I lost my virginity when I was eighteen years old after I'd sworn to myself and my father, I would wait until I was married. You see, I was raised in a very strict, Catholic, home. My father was a Bible geek, and he'd often wake me out of my sleep quoting verses pertaining to my virtue, that would often scare and annoy me. Nevertheless, I had every intention of maintaining my celibacy until I married my husband. But, all of that came to an end one Friday night in Atlanta, Georgia.

Not only were my parents extremely religious, but they were also racist, and had raised me to believe all races were supposed to stick to their own kind, and not mix with those that are not of your pigment. They instilled in me that white men were the most superior and that I was only allowed to date and marry one of them. I was from a very small town in Georgia and had never even seen that of another race, until I moved away to Atlanta, Georgia for college.

If you haven't guessed it, I am a Caucasian female. I am five feet two inches tall, with blue eyes, blonde hair, and double D breasts that I inherited from my mother. I have just enough backside to draw looks from men. But, not nearly as much ass as I've seen in Atlanta since I've been going to college here. So, back to the loss of my virginity.

One Friday night, about three weeks after I'd settled into my dorm room. My best friend Amy wanted to celebrate her twenty-first birthday at a club called, *Quest*. It was about nine o'clock in the evening when she came into our room with a big smile on her face.

"Sara, get dressed, you're going to come and celebrate my birthday with me. It's going to be so awesome. Just you wait." She opened the closet door in our room and pulled her blouse over her head. Then dropped her tight skirt to the floor, after wiggling out of it.

Amy was a well-developed woman. She was twenty-one, with a nice sized rack, and an ass that drove most of the guys on campus crazy. There were barely any places that we'd go where the men didn't fawn all over her. Like me, she was born and raised in the same town. Her family had been just as religious and racist as mine. In fact, her father and my father were best friends and hunting buddies. They shared the same beliefs on almost everything. Amy and I met in the first grade and had been best friends ever since. She knew everything about me, and I thought I knew everything about her, until this night.

I'd been studying for an upcoming quiz when she stormed into our room. I took my reading glasses off my nose and pushed my laptop forward on the study table. "What birthday? Your birthday was three weeks ago."

She pulled a red skirt dress from the closet and laid it out on the bed, then unhooked her bra from the front. "That wasn't a real birthday party. We celebrated that with our folks. No, I want a real live birthday celebration day, well night, because it's almost ten." She pulled her panties down her thighs and kicked them next to the bed and stood in front of me with her hands on her shapely hips. "Well, are you gonna come or what?"

She trailed her hand down her pussy mound, onto the surface of her hairless pussy. The fingers split the lips. I watched them open in front of me and felt a tingle go through my middle. Even though, I'd never gone all the way with a guy. Amy and I had been playing around together ever since we were eight years old and curious. Our sleepovers had been the best back then. As soon as we were in either her room, or mine, with the door locked, it was anything goes, and I have to admit a lot of things went, and we tried it all.

Seeing her standing there in front of me in her nude state was taking me back to our childhood. I felt myself getting moist. I crossed one of my thighs over the other one, causing my short nightgown to rise above my hips. I sighed, trying not to look down at her sex lips, but it was nearly impossible. "I'm not even dressed, besides, where do you want to go?"

She walked over to me, with her hands between her legs. "Gosh, Sara, I discovered this really cool club called Quest. It has some of the hunkiest guys there. You're going to love it, trust me." She smiled and grabbed my hand, putting it between her thighs. "You see how swollen I am from just thinking about that place?"

I rubbed her lips and squeezed them together with my fingers. Her pussy lips were hot and swollen. Traces of her juices were all over them already. I couldn't believe that the thought of a club could get my best friend so riled up.

"What's so good about this place? How are you so turned on by it and we aren't even there yet?"

She lifted her foot, and placed it between my now spread legs, right on the chair. "I need you, Sara. Seriously, I'm throbbing down there. Play with me like you used to when we were little. Do you remember?" She held her lips open for me and closed her eyes.

I sucked two fingers into my mouth and slid them into her nice and slow. I laid my cheek against her stomach. "Yes, I remember. Those nights were everything. Our little panties were thrown to the side of the bed, under the covers, kissing, and playing between each other's legs. It was everything!" I kissed her stomach breathlessly as I immediately became aroused replaying those images in my head. I fingered her as fast as I could.

"Uh-mmm-uh-Sara! I feel like we're little again!" She humped into my fingers moaning loudly. She kissed my lips and dug her nails into my shoulder blades before coming all over my hand while licking my neck at the same time.

I sucked my fingers into my mouth as I watched her make her way into the bathroom, heading for the shower. "I swear you're going to have a kick ass time. Trust me on this."

Two hours later, and with a joint of weed in my system, we wound up in the parking lot of Quest. The first thing I noticed was the sounds of the music coming from inside of the club. It wasn't like any music I'd ever listened to or heard before. It sounded like rap, or the music my father always told me belonged to the Devil. He'd said if ever I heard it, I was supposed to cover my ears or evil spirits would connect themselves to me.

At hearing this music, I became nervous and covered my ears as I stepped out of the car. Amy walked around from the driver's side with a look of irritation on her face.

"What's your problem? You look like a freaking idiot, right now." She pulled one of my hands down and looked around the big parking lot.

"That's the Devil's music. My dad says evil spirits will get on me if I listen to that crap."

The second thing I noticed was that all the cars in the parking lot seemed to have some sort of flashy hubcaps on them, along with weird paint jobs I'd never seen at a car dealership, and they looked real expensive. I was starting to think that the short, blue skirt and white halter I wore wasn't good enough for such a place that catered to customers who had to be rich in order to have afforded those cars. I felt insecure.

Amy frowned. "Will you stop it?" She looked over her shoulder as two short Black girls walked past us with skirts so short and tight, I could make out the bottom halves of their jiggling butt cheeks. They looked in our direction and turned their noses up, then walking toward the entrance of the club.

I was really starting to feel weird. "Wait a minute, Amy, what color people are in this club?"

"Look, Sara, that doesn't matter. All you need to worry about is having a good time. Fuck what our fathers taught us about different races of people. Because they were wrong. We're all equal, let's go in here, and have fun."

"But I've never been around any other race. If there are Blacks in there, I'm going to freak out. My dad said that—"

"Sara, shut the fuck up! Your dad was a nut job, and so was mine. They aren't here, it's just us. Now come on, and don't screw up my birthday celebration. I'll never forgive you if you do."

I lowered my head. "Okay, I promise I won't. But, don't leave my side. I'm going to be scared. You can't undo lifelong teachings in one night."

* * *

I sucked the Tequila up my straw, I was nervous and feeling so uncomfortable as I watched Amy dance with one black guy after the next. They rubbed all over her booty, squeezing it, a few pulled her skirt up so high, I was able to see their fingers playing between her thighs. Even though the club was dimly lit, it didn't stop me from being able to make all of that out. I sat at our table, constantly checking the time on my phone, ready to leave. The music was so loud it was giving me a headache.

After being on the dance floor for a full hour, Amy staggered back to our table with a huge smile on her face. Her eyes were barely opened. "You're such a party pooper. I can't believe you aren't dancing with some of these fine black men. They are the shit!" She slumped down next to me and drank from my glass of Tequila.

"Amy, it's going on two thirty. Let's get out of here, you should be all danced out," I said looking around the club.

It didn't look like the party was ending any time soon. That worried me because I was ready to leave.

Before Amy could give me an answer, two dark-skinned black men approached the table with bottles of expensive Champagne in their hands. One of them tapped Amy on the shoulder. He was about six feet two inches tall. He wore a black beater that was conformed to his chest. His arms were huge and glistening. He had a short haircut, that looked like a curly Mohawk. He smelled quite nice, as much as I hated to admit it. I could hear my father in my head hollering for me to run away from the pair and call the police.

"Say, baby, ain't you the lil' white girl that was just on the dance floor with all of that ass?" He asked, looking into Amy's blue eyes with his own.

Amy smiled. "Yes, that was me. What did you like it or something?" She looked up at him and crossed her thighs.

He laughed. "Check dis out, Shawty, me and my mans from New York. We fucking around in Atlanta shooting a few music videos. With all that ass, you can definitely star in one of my joints. What you think about that?" He asked, smiling down on her.

I didn't know what he was talking about. I was terrified, and ready to run, screaming for the law. All I heard was shooting, and I was shaking in my three-inch heels.

Amy stood up and grabbed his wrist. "Let's talk about this over here. You've surely piqued my interest, though."

He slid his arm around her lower back, then under her skirt moving all around underneath it. The next thing I knew, we were back at their hotel, and I was scared for my life. After the door had closed, and we'd been drinking for what seemed like an hour, Amy walked over to where I was seated on the couch and pulled me to my feet by my right hand.

"Come on, I want you to dance with, Travis. He's really feeling you." She pulled me toward the bedroom where both men were rolling cigars full of weed."

"Amy, what are you talking about. I've never danced with a black guy before. I'm begging you, don't do this!"

"Girl, chill, it's okay. They won't bite unless we tell them too. Hey, Travis, she can't wait to dance with you. You guys go ahead, while me and Drake do our thing."

Travis stood up and slid his arms around my body. I could feel his stomach muscles through his shirt. His big arms enveloped me and made me feel like a little girl. His scent was intoxicating. "Hey, there lil' lady, it's okay. You ain't gotta be afraid of me." He kissed me on the neck sending a tingle down my spine.

I shivered. "I'm not afraid of you. I've just never danced with a black guy before, that's it." I looked over his shoulder to see Amy and Drake making out.

She was straddled atop his lap, while his hands rubbed all over her ass. I could see from that distance that her pink nipples were rock hard, and poking against her top.

"Aw, well let me say thank you for allowing for me to be your first." He kissed my neck, and grabbed a hold of my ass, forcing me to his body. I could feel the long length of his penis along my stomach. When his teeth went into my neck, I shivered again. "Wait, what are you doing, I thought we were just dancing?" I asked as my voice broke.

I didn't know what was coming over me. But, the feel of his big hands fondling my ass was turning me on like never before. Not only was I terrified, but I was also intrigued by the forbidden.

"We are just dancing, this how black dudes dance." He pulled my skirt above my waist and slid his fingers under the band of my thong separating my butt cheeks. I felt them graze over my hairless mound and shuddered from his gentle touches.

I peered over at Amy as she pulled down her top and squeezed her tits together for Drake to suck them. He slid his pants down his thighs, and off. Amy reached under them, pulled out his penis through the hole of his boxers and stroked it up and down. It looked like a brown cucumber. My eyes were wide open. I couldn't believe its length and girth.

'Are all black men hung like this?' I thought.

Travis turned me around to face him. He slid his hand into the front of my panties and rubbed my hairless sex. He kissed my lips, softly at first, then in a demanding way. "You are way finer than your friend. I didn't even notice her when y'all walked into the club. All I saw was you. I've never seen a woman as fine as you in my life." He sucked on my neck as he sneakily slid a finger up my box.

I stood on my tippy toes, as a moan escaped me. "Thank you." Was all I managed to get out, as he continued to invade my body.

My whole life, I'd always heard how pretty and perfect, Amy was. No one had ever paid any attention to me when she was in the same room. Now here was this forbidden man, telling me that even though, he'd noticed her, all he saw was me. My guard fell as soon as those words left his lips.

He picked me up and sat me on the edge of the bed where Amy was lowering herself onto Drake's penis, in the reverse cowgirl position. She leaned all the way over with her pink ass in the air, twerking hard on Drake's huge penis. He smacked her on it, then fingered her asshole, while she screamed at the top of her lungs and rode him faster and faster, with her titties bouncing on her chest.

Travis knelt between my legs and licked the crotch of my wet panties. He yanked the material to the side and sucked both of my lips into his mouth. The sounds were too much for me. I arched my back and opened my thighs wider to give him better access.

I could hear my father's voice in my head, calling me a whore. Telling me, I was going to hell for screwing around with this color of a man. As much as it scared me to think about what my dad would do if he found out, the more it turned me on. That coupled with the screams coming from Amy's mouth. I couldn't see what they were doing any longer, but the bed was going haywire. Travis peeled my lips back and ran his tongue in circles around my clitoris. When he slid a finger deep into my hole, I came all over his mouth.

"Ah-Travis-Travis!" I couldn't stop shaking. I felt like all the pleasure I'd been deprived of by men had come rushing to me at that moment.

After I came, he stood up, and sucked all over my neck, while kicking his pants and boxers off. He fell between my legs and forced my thighs apart. I could feel his huge penis throbbing against my mound. It felt like a hot log of meat.

"I gotta have some of this pussy, white girl. You got me turned all the way up," he growled deep within his throat.

He licked all over my neck. I tried to push him off me. "No, you don't understand. I've never-I've never—" My nails dug into his back, as his teeth went into my neck hitting my spot.

I couldn't let this be my first time. I couldn't lose my virginity to a black man. It couldn't happen this way. My father would kill me. I tried to push him away, but all I could feel was solid muscle, and a rock-hard penis, that felt as if it were too long to fit into a human being.

He rubbed his dick up and down in between the fold of my pussy before the big head started to penetrate me. "I gotta have some of this. Damn this pussy hot, and you're so fucking gorgeous." He sucked my neck. "Open these thighs," he demanded

I don't know why I did it, but I opened my thighs wide. As soon as I did, he cocked back and slammed his penis as far into me as he possibly could. I felt him tear through all my barriers.

The pain shot through my middle. "Aahhh-fuck!" I whimpered.

By the third plunge from him, I was in ecstasy. His big dick went in and out of me at full speed. Hitting spots inside of my body, I didn't even know could be hit. I couldn't stop shaking.

"Damn, you tight, this pussy tight," He moaned, picking up speed.

He pushed my breasts together and sucked them through my see-through bra. I yanked my bra under my titties for him. "There they are, suck my nipples. Oh my, God, suck them! It feels so good. Take me, harder!" I cried as he pounded away between my thighs.

He pulled on my long pink nipples with his lips, smacking loudly. Then he would suck all over my neck. "You're so beautiful. You got some good ass pussy, white girl. Tell me you love this black dick. Tell me!" He slammed into me so hard that I sat upright and fell back to the bed again.

"I love it, I love your black dick! I love it, aw fuck, I love it!" I screamed cumming all over his pole. My eyes rolled into the back of my head as my orgasm ripped through me.

"I knew it, I knew it, I knew you would! This fresh pussy so wet! I'm cumming, bitch! I'm cumming all in this shit!" He crashed into me ten quick times. Then I felt him released spurts of semen into my womb. That alone, caused me to break into another orgasm. I imagined my father walking into the room, catching us in the act. I could only imagine what he would say and do.

I felt dirty, yet free at the same time. Before it was all said and done, Travis found out I'd been a virgin. He fucked me as hard as he could from the back while pulling my hair, then he made me eat Amy's pussy in front of him and Drake. I came so many times I wound up passing out.

When I came to, both men were fucking Amy. Travis was in her pussy, while, Drake fucked her ass. Then it was her turn to eat me until I came. Drake and Travis took turns helping me fall in love with not only their skin complexions but their race of men in general. It's been two years since I had my first taste of black dick and I haven't looked back since then.

My Sister's Husband

Three weeks ago, I made the biggest mistake of my l life when I slept with my sister's husband and children's father. Even as I sit and write this, I cannot help but lower my head in shame. My sister, Kim, is my best friend. She and I have always been extremely close. We grew up in a household where we share two older brothers. Our parents were divorced two years after she, the youngest, was born. The children in our household were caught in the middle of a custody battle. It ended with Kim and me, living with our mother full time, and our brothers went to live with our father who stayed an hour away in Miami, Florida.

After high school, I went off to college at Clarke University, to become a child psychologist. I have always had a passion for caring for children and the elderly. It was during one of my Spring breaks where I'd made the mistake of sleeping with my sister's husband, Vincent.

Vincent and Kim had gotten married two years after she'd moved out of our mother's home. It was also around this time that she'd found out, she was pregnant with my niece. Prior to her pregnancy, Kim had always said she was going to be a Social Worker. That she wanted to work with families who were struggling to get ahead in life. Most importantly, she wanted to protect the children within those families. I understood where she was coming from because I held the same passion for families and children as well. So, we clicked with our future goals, and paths we were destined to take until she became pregnant.

After she became pregnant with my niece, she dropped out of school and became very distant towards me. Where we'd usually talk every single day. It boiled down to maybe twice a month, if even.

As the months went by, I started to miss my sister more and more. We would connect on Facebook, and through Instagram, but that wasn't enough for me. I had to see her in the physical. After all, she was only a few hundred miles away in Miami, while I resided in Georgia. After nagging her for weeks on end, she finally agreed that I could spend my Spring break with her and her family. She said, she'd try her best to make it my best stay ever, but I should know that she took night classes five days a week. When she first told me that I was saddened because I knew it would take away from our time together. Then again, I was happy just to be able to see her and spend some time with her. Beggars couldn't be choosers.

I packed my things one Wednesday afternoon and headed for the sunny city of Miami. My sister met me at the Airport, she was holding up a big sign that said: *'Baby Sister Wanted! Will pay in food stamps.'* It cracked me up so much, I was still laughing while I hugged her, with my luggage in tow.

When we got in her Lincoln Navigator, she looked over at me and smiled. "Girl, if I would have known, you'd gotten this damn fine. Ain't no way in hell I would have let you come down here. I guess that strip club you're working at also has an aerobics room, huh?" She laughed pulling out into traffic.

I blushed. "I didn't even know you knew, I was working at the King of Diamonds. Who told you?" I asked avoiding eye contact with her.

I was hoping she wasn't looking down on me. For some reason, my sister's opinion of me had always mattered way more than it should have.

She shrugged her shoulders. "Don't worry about it. How much money you be making working up in there. I see you got on a Burberry skirt dress. You're wearing red bottoms with your little yellow toes all done up. Bitch, you look like money!"

I felt a little uneasy. One because she sounded immature for her age of Thirty, and secondly, I didn't want to discuss my lifestyle. I was there to see her, and for me, that was all that mattered. "I do okay. But I don't want to talk about that. How is Asia?" Asia was my little niece, she was a spitting image of my sister.

"Getting bigger and staying on my damn nerves as usual. If you want, you can take her back with you. I'll send for her in a few years." I expected her to laugh, but she held a stone face. Once again, I felt uneasy.

"I'm sure, Vincent, wouldn't approve of that." I adjusted myself in my seat and pulled my short skirt down over my thick thighs.

I couldn't get the material to stop riding up. I'd gained about three pounds. All of it went to my ass and thighs. I was what you would call strapped. Five feet five inches, a hundred and thirty pounds, light-skinned, with reddish brown hair, and light freckles. No matter how much I ate right and worked out my thighs and ass did what they wanted to do, and I was okay with that.

"Don't get me started on, Vincent. I'm just not as happy as I used to be. I think Asia changed a lot for us. Ever since her birth we've been on a downward spiral. I don't know what to do. We've been arguing a lot lately, and I guess I should have warned you before you came.

I just wanted to see you so bad, I feared it would have turned you off from coming. And I seriously need to have another adult in the house outside of him. I feel like I'm losing my mind. I'm not even kidding. I promise to try and make this the best stay for you, I possibly can. I just wanted to give you a heads up."

"So, what should I do? Should I not say anything to him or something? Like how is his personality now? I haven't seen him in a long time."

"I don't know. He's been angry a whole lot. When I told him, you were coming all he did was grunt. Just try and stay out of his way. We'll do our own thing. Hey, dad was a bit of a jerk, but that never stopped us from doing us, right?" She asked placing her hand on my thigh.

I smiled, "Yeah, you're right. It's all about us connecting anyway. I won't let Vincent ruin that, no matter how much of a buzz kill he intends on being."

* * *

I stepped into the living room of my sister's three-bedroom home and took my Red Bottoms off my feet. My toes sank into the white carpet. The aroma coming from the kitchen had my stomach growling like an angry bear. I dropped my suitcase next to me and closed the door behind me.

"I'll be right back. I'ma go and see if Asia is awake yet when I left, she wasn't. You'll be staying in the guest room, right down that hallway. It's all set up for you," Kim said heading up the stairs.

I grabbed my things, and headed down the hallway, into the guest room. As I placed the suitcases on the hardwood floor, I felt a presence behind me. I was bent over with my skirt rose up on my thighs. I almost jumped out of my skin when I looked over my shoulder and saw Vincent's six-foot-four-inch frame blocking the doorway. He wore a tight, white cotton T-shirt. I could see his eight packed abs through it, along with the swells of his chest muscles. He smelled like Bulgari cologne. His dreads were neatly twisted, and his lining was crisp and defined.

"Yo', I know that ain't, Free, looking this damn fine? Girl, if you don't stand yo' ass up and give me a hug." He stepped around my body and pulled me into his frame, hugging me tightly. I could really feel all of him, including the part of him that I shouldn't have but couldn't deny its presence.

I hugged him timid at first, but as I felt his grip tightened, so did my own. "Hey, Vincent. How have you been, big bro?" I asked trying to pry myself out of his embrace before my sister caught us like that. I didn't know how she'd react, and I didn't want to find out.

His hands brushed over my lower back, then slightly over my ass, before he stepped back, and looked down on me. "Yo', I'm good, but look at you, though. I swear you look like a million bucks. Look at this curly hair and shit. How did you get this thick? You was skinny as hell the last time I saw you." He held my right arm up and drank in the sights of my body with his eyes. He looked angry like he really couldn't understand how I'd gotten so bad. My eyes went to his crotch, I saw a slight bulge there. I blushed, I couldn't believe, I was having such an effect on a grown man. My sister's man at that.

In the club when men fawned over me, I found it creepy. But, seeing Vincent look me over with lust in his eyes was doing something to my body I couldn't really explain. He dared to kiss my cheek before I could even respond. Once again, his hand brushed over my backside.

I looked into his eyes and shrugged my shoulders. "I couldn't stay a little girl forever, could I?"

His big hands slid around my waist, and cupped my ass, squeezing the cheeks. "Hell naw, you couldn't. You're all woman now. I ain't gon' be able to st—" He broke away from me when Kim called my name. I could hear the stairs creaking as she made her way down them, with Asia's hand in hers. "Look, I can't take my eyes off you. We need to talk and catch up when she goes to school tonight. Is that cool?" He asked, looking over his shoulder expecting Kim to enter the hallway any second now.

I nodded my head. "That's fine."

I could feel my nipples poking against my bra. Did he just squeeze my ass? Most importantly, had I just let him without saying a word? Was I going to tell my sister? That would have been the right thing to do, right?

* * *

After spending some time with Asia and catching up with Kim. I took the time to set up the guest room to my level of comfort. By that time, it was eight thirty at night, and Kim had to get to school. It turned out that the night school she went to also had a daycare facility. As much as I begged her to let Asia stay with me, she declined. She said the teachers at the daycare were teaching Asia her ABC's and how to tie her shoe. That she couldn't afford for her to miss a day, so that was that. She got herself, and Asia dressed then headed out the door with her phone in her hand. "I'll be back in three hours. Try and get some sleep. We have a big day tomorrow. I wanna show you everything you've missed since you've been away from Miami."

I assured her I would, closed the door, took a deep breath, and yawned. I could feel my energy slowly slipping away from me. The effects of the day were finally starting to take their toll on me. I walked away from the door, headed to my bedroom.

Vincent appeared at the top of the stairs and rushed down them. "Is she gone?" He asked.

I stopped in my tracks. He was shirtless, his body was popping, he had muscles on top of muscles. He looked like a caramel skinned model, and his basketball shorts showcased the indention of his tool.

"Yeah, she said she had to get there right away. That she was already running late. I'm about to hit the hay. I'll see you in the morning." I yawned again and tried not to look down at his print.

He blocked my path and shook his head. "Naw, you ain't about to leave me up all by myself. I thought we was gon' catch up and get to know one another better?" He pulled me by the waist until I crashed into him.

I yelped. Damn the way he snatched me up had me feeling some type of way. "I need to rest for a little while, Vincent. I been up since three o'clock this morning, I'm beat." I tried to wiggle out of his grasp. He held me firmer, my lips wound up against his neck.

He kissed my forehead. "You got me going through it, Free. Look at all this ass, Ma." He cupped my booty, then slid his hands under my skirt, touching my naked skin. "I can't focus with you in this house, my head's spinning. He ran his hands into my crease. A finger played over the mound of my sex through the panties.

I pushed him away. "Boy, if you don't stop, I'ma tell my sister on yo' ass. You know she'll snap." I rolled my eyes, as I felt my juices leaking out of me. "Now, like I said, I'm going to sleep. I'll holler at you in the morning."

I turned around to walk away from him. He grabbed me by the arm and tossed me over the arm of the couch. Taking the hem of my skirt, pulling up to my waist. "I just wanna taste you. You done got way too fucking bad. Besides, I've always had a thing for you." He kneeled down, and stuck his face between my thighs, sucking up and down them while his hands rested on my cheeks. When I felt the band of my panties being pulled to the side, I got weak in the knees.

"Vincent, chill out. I can't do my sister like this. It ain't right, and you know it." I tried to fight out of his grasp with all the resistance I could muster. I knew what we were about to do was wrong. But when his lips sucked on my clitoris, my teenaged hormones took over. I threw my head back and moaned. "Stop Vincent!" But I was praying he didn't.

"I'm sorry, Free. I can't help myself, you just so fucking fine!" He spread my booty cheeks and licked in between them. His tongue was like a mini penis, darting in and out of my back door, while he pinched my clitoris. I didn't know how much more I could take.

I spread my thighs and bit into my bottom lip. My eyes were closed as tight as I could get them. I could feel his entire face in between my legs. He was licking up and down my slit. It made me wonder if my sister had ever found herself bent over the couch by him like I was. When two of his fingers entered me from the back, I came all over them, biting into the couch pillow.

Vincent stood up and pulled down his shorts. His big dick stood out from his body like a baseball bat. "Come on, Free. Let me see how you get down, Ma! I ain't gon' say shit, my word is bond." He grabbed a hand full of my hair and helped me kneel in front of him. He continued to stroke his dick up and down.

I don't know, what got into me, or why I did what I did next. But the next thing I knew he was in my mouth, and I was deep throating that long pipe, while his fingers twisted my curls. I'd suck him all the way to his balls, then pull my mouth all the way backward, before sucking him down again. The sounds coming from his body was driving me up the wall. His toes curled, as he sucked into my mouth. I continued to handle my business, right there in the middle of my sister's living room floor.

It was all wrong, I knew I was bogus. I slid my hand between my thighs and squeezed my lips together. I was squatted down with my thighs wide open. My juices were all over my ankles, and still pouring out of me.

Vincent cocked back and lunged forward. I could feel the veins along his shaft. "I'm about to cum, Free. I'm finna cum, aw fuck, Free!" He groaned and began to shoot his seed into my mouth.

I continued to suck, and swallow everything that came out of him. Even after he finished, I couldn't take my lips away. Before I knew it, he was back, hard, and pulsating in my mouth.

I popped him out and stroked it up and down. "You know we bogus right? My sister gon' kill me when she finds out." I could taste his cum on my tongue, and in the back of my throat.

He grabbed me by the hair once again. I stood up, and he picked me up. I wrapped my legs around him. "Put this dick in you, Free. Come on, if we gon' cross them lines you gon' have to do some of the dirty work too. Now, I know you wanna fuck me just as bad as I wanna fuck you. But, ain't shit happening unless you put this piece inside of you." He held me up it the air and kissed all over my lips. His fingers ran in and out of my pussy. I licked his neck and sucked on his earlobe. "Don't make me do this," I whispered. "Please don't make me do this." I took hold of his dick and placed the head at my opening. My hot lips tried to suck him inside of me.

"It's good, Free. I want some of this body too. Just put me in, let's do this shit together. It can be our little secret!" He licked my neck. "I'ma fuck the shit out of you. I promise!"

I moaned. I loved my sister, but the whore in me took over. I popped his big dick head into my tight lil' hole and put my tongue in his ear. "Fuck me, Vincent! Fuck me, please!"

He pulled me all the way down on his dick and slid me back up it. Before I knew it, I was being thrown into the air, and he was dicking me down. I could feel him forcing my insides to make room for him as he battered his way inside of me. I wrapped my arms around his neck and trapped his juicy lips with my own, moaning into his mouth.

"It's so good, it's so good! Fuck me, bro. Fuck me, shit. You feel so good," I cried out in ecstasy.

I didn't see how my sister could stand to argue with a man with so much pipe. Had he been mines, there would have never been room for arguing, only screwing.

He fell to the floor with me. His hips were working overtime. His dick sawed in and out of my opening, hitting the deepest regions in my womb. "Damn, Free damn! Damn-Free-aw shit, Free! I'm cumming, Shawty-I'm cumming!" He quickly pulled out of me, flipped me over, and decorated my ass with his seed, scalding my skin, feeling like hot candle wax.

I was so close before he'd pulled out. I reached between my legs and thumbed my clitoris. "Vincent, you gotta finish me off. I gotta cum, please let me cum!" I begged, opening my lips wide for him to see.

He flipped me onto my back and forced me into a ball, then pulled down my top to expose my titties, sucking on both hard nipples. "Damn, this body something else. Look at these pretty ass titties." He slid back into my pussy, pummeling me so hard tears escaped me. I started to shake, I felt my climax building from deep within the pits of my stomach. My vision went blurry, and I could feel him hammering away at my middle. I arched my back, giving him better leverage and screamed as loud as I could, cumming harder than I ever had in all my life. That only enticed him, motivating him to go into overdrive. I yelped as I felt his teeth penetrate my neck. His cum splashed on my walls like paint.

My body jerked. Sweat poured down the side of my face. I could not believe what we'd just done. As his dick deflated and fell out of my hole, my conscious began to kick in. I slid from underneath him, and stood up, "Oh! Shit!"

Standing in the hallway, about twenty feet away from where we were, was Kim. She had a scowl on her face, and both fists balled up.

I pulled down my skirt and backed away with my hands at chest level. "Kim, wait a minute I can explain."

Vincent stood up and smacked me on the ass. "Ain't nothing to explain." He looked over at her and lowered his eyes. "I bet you won't have no problem giving me that divorce now, will you?"

Mommy Issues

I've been attracted to older women ever since I was old enough to know men and women were different. I think the finest women walking this earth are thirty years and older. I am eighteen, and I don't find any of the women my age attractive in the least bit. I don't know why that is, but it just is. I didn't get my first chance to actually sleep with an older woman until a month ago. I had just graduated from high school, and to celebrate, me and my right-hand man, Nitty thought it would be cool, to get a couple bottles of Patron, and an ounce of Loud, so we could get wasted.

A couple of females from our school wanted to tag along and I was cool with that. I mean what man wouldn't want to have a few dames around after he got turnt up. So, me, my man Nitty, and two of his female friends jumped in my Monte Carlo SS and headed to Rock Point. It was an area in Brooklyn, New York where most of the teenagers from our school, and surrounding schools went to neck with the hotties from school. It was like a little bridge that overlooked the city from above. We'd park our cars, then turnt up, while our trunks knocked, and the inside of the whip got steamed up if you know what I mean.

This particular night, after blowing half a zip of Loud, and getting toasty off the bottles, my man Nitty, got sick and started throwing up everywhere, along with one of the females he'd brought along with us. I don't know if he'd drank too much, or maybe he was too high, but before we could get at the shorties in the back seat, our night had been ruined. I wound up dropping the ladies off first, then making my way in the direction of Nitty's crib, with him laying against the passenger's door with a moist towel draped over his face.

"Say, Son, my mom's about to flip, Kid. I promised her before I went out that I wasn't gon' fuck with them bottles. Now, look at me. I don't feel like hearing her mouth, right now, word up." He grabbed a half of bottle of Patron and started guzzling it like a thirsty fish. After he finished, he burped and closed his eyes.

"Bruh, what the fuck is your problem. You just got done throwing up all over yourself! Now you drink some more," I snapped at him.

"Yo, fuck it, Dunn, she gon' be vexed anyway. I might as well get as drunk as I can, the damage is done." He wiped his face with the rag. Seconds later, I could hear him snoring so loud I wanted to punch him.

By the time, I pulled in front of his house, I'd already texted his mother. She was looking out of their big back window when I arrived. She came storming out of the house, with a burgundy robe tied tight around her perfect body. Man, when it came to sexy older women, Nitty's mother Pam was the epitome of sexy. She was five feet seven inches tall. I guessed about one thirty-five, with hazel eyes, and caramel skin, that popped like no other. She had these real big breasts that sagged a little to let you know they were real.

No matter what she wore she couldn't help, but expose her cleavage and on top of that, she had one of the most round and perfect asses I'd ever seen. She was in her late thirties, or early forties, but you could not tell by looking at her. She would put any twenty-year-old to shame, she was that bad. I don't think I pleasured myself to any female more than I did to her. Along with her beauty, she always smelled so damn good. I'd known her since I was two years old, I swear I can remember every bath she'd ever given me as a kid. Her and my mother were really good high school friends, so she'd been part of our lives forever.

She stormed down to the car and leaned into the passenger's window. The wind blew and sent her perfume in my direction. I inhaled and closed my eyes. Damn, she always smelled so good.

She grabbed a hold of Nitty's ear and pulled it. "Nitty! Nitty! Wake your ass up this instant!" She smacked him on the cheek. Nitty's head shook, but he continued to snore. The alcohol on his breath smelled bad. I wanted to get him out of my car before he stunk it up. Pam reached inside the window and tried to pop the lock.

"I'm finna whoop his lil' ass because he told me he wasn't going to be drinking that stuff. All a man has is his word. He's not gon' turn out to be a liar like his father. I refuse to let that happen." She jiggled the door handle and pulled it open.

Nitty fell out of the car onto the curb, snoring away. It was so funny I wanted to laugh, but the anger on her face told me that would have been a bad idea. I took off my seatbelt instead and came around the car, kneeling on the side of him.

"I'm sorry about this, Mrs. Parker. I'll carry him into the house that way we get him out of the street. Is that cool?" I asked looking up at her.

Her thick thighs were on display and with the wind blowing, I could smell all of her. Her scents were driving me up the wall. I could not believe this woman was this damn fine. She crossed her arms in front of her and rubbed her shoulders. "Well, it is chilly out here. And I don't want the neighbors all in my business. So, yeah, that'll be cool." She turned to walk back up the steps to her stoop, with her robe swaying in the wind.

I was praying the wind would send the material up just a little higher, so I could see what she was wearing underneath that robe. I felt myself getting hard just looking at her. I knew this night was going to be a rough one for me. Now, I was wishing I'd dropped off, Nitty's female friends last. That way I could have tried to talk one of them into giving me some. It didn't seem like it would have been a hard task. Both girls had already made it known that they were trying to get down. Fuck! I was regretting my decision to drop them off now.

Pam stopped on the top step of the stoop and looked over her shoulder at me. Just as the wind blew harshly through the night and sent her flimsy robe waving enough to expose the blue thongs that separated her caramel ass cheeks. She hurriedly pulled it back down, but it was too late. I had already seen the glory, and I was so hard I was hurting.

"Devin, will you hurry up, and get my baby inside?" She asked, before entering the Brownstone.

* * *

I got Nitty into his bed and even pulled his Jordan's off for him. The whole time he kept mumbling about his mother whooping his ass when she found out. He told me not to take him home. To let him spend a night at my crib, before he started snoring like a damn bear.

"You know it's your fault, right?" Pam said standing in the doorway with her arms folded.

I stood up and looked over at her. "What are you talking about?"

She told me to come here using her index finger and stepped out of the doorway. In seconds I was following behind her. I couldn't help but look down at that big booty as it swayed from right to left, in the tight robe. The more she walked the higher the robe rose until I could make out the bottom halves of her caramel ass cheeks. The bottoms were darker along the top of her thighs where her ass met her thighs. I felt my piece jump, I followed her into the living room. She sat down on the love seat and instructed me to sit on the couch across from her.

She crossed her thick thighs, and the robe raised so far on them that it virtually disappeared. She looked at me and smiled. "I should whoop your ass since he's too drunk to feel it. You're supposed to be setting a better example for him. You know he looks up you." She uncrossed her legs, only to cross them the other way. In doing so she flashed me a peek of her blue bikini panties.

My dick got so hard, I grabbed one of the small couch pillows and put it in my lap. I was so embarrassed and prayed she didn't know what was going on. "I can't make Nitty do nothing he don't want to do. Besides, we'll be off to college this fall. We were just celebrating." I refused to make eye contact with her. But, for some reason, my eyes kept going back to her thighs. I was hoping she'd opened them again, so I could see between them. This woman was fucking gorgeous.

She ran her tongue across her lips. "Devin, aren't I like a mother to you?" She asked uncrossing her legs, leaning back on the couch with them slightly apart. Her movement caused them to jiggle just a little bit. Her perfect toes sunk into the carpet with pink paint on them. Her legs were slightly ajar, and I could smell her more natural scent coupled with that of her perfume. It was like her pheromones were calling out to me.

"Of course, you're like my mother. I've known you all my life. You used to bathe me for God sakes." Even though, I was saying these words to her my eyes never left her gap. I could see how the panties were pulled tight against her sex. The lips were pressed up against the material, making themselves known. I was hoping I could taste her. I would have given anything to swallow her juices. I knew they would be sweet. Nitty never even crossed my mind.

She pinched the sides of her robe, and pulled it upward, opening her thighs wider. "Then if I'm like your mother, why you looking between my legs with that look in your eyes? See something you want, huh, son?"

I shuddered, as she opened her thighs wider, and pulled her panties to the side, then started running her finger up and down her wet slit. She slid the finger into her box a few times and pulled it out, holding it up to me. "Here you go."

I rushed to her side, fell to my knees, grabbed her wrist, and sucked the finger into my mouth. It tasted sweet just like I imagined, with a hint of salt. I licked all over the finger and moaned around it. My noises were loud in the front room.

She rubbed my crotch, then squeezed my dick. "Mmm, I don't remember this being this big, baby. I see you're all grown up now! Let me see you play wit' it while you look at me. We can't go any further than that, okay?" She pulled the sash on her robe, then opened it all the way to expose the fact that she was wearing a matching blue, see-through Victoria Secrets Bra. Her nipples were big, and brown, they stood out a half an inch. The way they stuck through the material looked as if they were trying to poke a hole in it. She took her left leg and draped it over the couch. She pulled her panties all the way to the side for me to see her treasures. Then took two fingers and rubbed them up and down her groove, coating them with her juices.

I stood up and dropped my pants and boxers at the same time. I started stroking my pipe, looking directly at her meaty, bald pussy. I imagined what it would feel like to be balls deep inside of her. I was already close to cumming. My hand was a blur up and down my dick, I needed to release my seed.

She rubbed up and down my thigh. "My have you grown. You're almost a man." She squeezed her titties together, pinching the nipples. "Come a lil' closer baby. Stand between my legs, so I can feel all over you." She inhaled, running her hands all over my stomach, and along my waistline.

I was so horny, I couldn't stop pumping my dick. I dared to take my hand and rub between her legs. Every time I tried to touch her pussy, she pushed my hand away. But I would try again, I wanted to touch it so bad I felt like I was going crazy.

"Mrs. Parker, please, let me touch it. I need to touch it so bad," I groaned and kneeled down rubbing my hard dick up and down her thick thigh leaving a trail of pre-cum. "Please!"

She shook her head and slipped two fingers into her pussy. "No baby, you're like my son. I can't let you do that," She moaned and arched her back.

I rubbed my dick up and down her thigh again, and reached for her pussy, pumping her fingers that were buried deep inside of her. I sucked her nipple through the bra.

She groaned and pushed me away from her. "That's it since you can't follow the rules you gotta go. Come on." She stood up and walked toward the door closing her robe.

I pulled my pants up, and my dick stood straight up along my stomach, throbbing against my belly button. "Mrs. Parker, I'm sorry. Please, I won't do it again. Just let me finish, I'm so close," I whimpered.

She shook her head and pulled her panties back over her pussy mound. "I'm sorry, son, I can't. Besides, I would have felt bad to do that to your mother anyway. I practically helped raise you boy." She pointed to the door. "Out!"

I lowered my head and sighed. "Okay." I walked to the door and unlocked it. "Tell, Nitty, I'll holler at him tomorrow. You have a nice night."

"I'll do that, and you have one too, drive safely. When you get home tell your mother I said, hey. Huh, give me a hug before you go." She held out her arms for me.

I reluctantly walked into them, with my dick sticking straight out in front of me leading the way. It made it to her before I did.

She moaned and wiggled her hips into it. "Damn boy, yeah, you gotta go, or I'ma make a mistake." She tried to take a step back, but I slid my hands down, and took a hold of her ass, pressing her into my hard-on. "Let me go, Devin, what's the matter with you?"

I slid my hand under her ass, and into her panties from the back. "I been wanting to fuck you my whole life. I ain't never seen nobody as fine as you. I'm taking this pussy!"

I backed her up against the door, and sucked on her neck, at the same time, while pulling her robe wide open, and squeezing her breasts in my hands.

"Watch your mouth, you better respect me," She moaned with her eyes closed. She held her arms out at her sides. "You better-better hurry up before my husband gets home. I can't believe you're doing this to me." She kissed my lips and ran her tongue over them.

I had my fingers in the leg holes of her panties rubbing along her silky mound. I picked her up and fell to the floor with her. "I need some of this cat, Mrs. Parker. I won't be long, I just need it so bad." I yanked her panties off her in one hard tug. Then ripped open her bra.

Her titties spilled out into the palms of my hands. Both nipples were fully erect. I sucked the first one, then the other into my mouth, while I thought back on all the times, I'd lusted off her bosom. I'd be over visiting with Nitty, then she'd walk past me with her nipples poking through her shirt, and big booty jiggling in a short skirt. The next thing I knew, I was in the bathroom beating my meat with my eyes closed tight trying to recreate what I'd just seen. It was very rare that I'd come over to Nitty's crib, without having to go to the bathroom to relieve myself over his mother. She was too much.

She wrapped her thick thighs around my waist and humped into my hard penis. "I want you to fuck me, Devin. Put this young meat in my pussy. I want it, son. I want you just as bad as you want me. Can you do that for, Mommy?" She purred and squeezed my dick again.

I don't know why, but every time she referred to herself as my mother, it sent tingles all through my body. It made me want to fuck her as hard as I could. I still couldn't believe I had Mrs. Parker on her back, begging me to screw her. If it was a dream, I would have killed whoever woke me up from it. I kicked my pants and boxers all the way off, and put her legs on my shoulders, ready to dive in that juicy pussy. I sucked all over her lips, our tongues wrestled while we breathed heavily into each other's mouths.

She reached between our bodies, and gripped my dick like a flashlight, placing the big head on her opening. "Fuck Mommy, baby. Do it to me hard. Don't play wit' my kitty." She dug her nails into my shoulder.

I slammed forward and implanted my piece deep into her womb. I let out a gush of air, her hotness sucked me inside of her. The walls seemed to squeeze my piece in its grip. I started to shudder from just being inside of this woman I'd lusted after my entire life. I leaned forward and delivered long strokes, still in unbelief that I was fucking her.

"Mrs. Parker, damn, it's so good!" I managed to get out.

Her pretty toes were on my shoulders. "Yes-yes! Do it, baby. Do it to me harder," She moaned, with her mouth wide open.

She hugged me into her embrace, and we connected as one. I started plunging into her body with everything I had, while she whimpered in my ear and egged me on. Her juices caused my pubic hairs to curl up. She leaked all over me. The feeling was so intense I was on the verge of cumming already. I couldn't help it, no matter how hard I tried to hold back, it was coming.

"I'm cumming, Momma. I'm cumming hard, Mrs. Parker. Aw-man!" I slammed into her and began to spurt my seed deep into her womb.

She tried to sit all the way up, dug her nails into my back, and came all over my dick as she whimpered in my ear. "Did you like Momma, baby? Tell me you loved it." She stuck her tongue into my ear and began rubbing my back.

All I could do was shudder and squeeze her tighter, while my seed leaked out of me and into her. "I loved it."

She slipped from my embrace and sucked her juices off my dick, while her breasts rested on my thighs and her nipples poking me. "Long as you can keep this secret baby, me and you can live out some of deepest fantasies. I know you have Mommy issues, but I have some of my own. Now lay back and let me get up here."

Ca$h & Company

Rental Agreement

Damn, I couldn't believe I was going to have to be late with my rent again. I continued to look at the screen on my phone, confirming that there had been no new deposit into my PayPal account. Even though my baby's father swore up and down he was going to be sending his child support by today. I was so angry, I wanted to throw my phone against the wall and break it into a million pieces. But that wouldn't have solved anything. I sat on the couch in my living room with my head lowered, and hands covering my face. I didn't know what to do. I couldn't call, my mother and ask to borrow more money. She'd just given me a five-thousand-dollar loan less than a month earlier to help with the costs of opening my hair salon.

Although things were set to launch without a glitch, the doors had not opened. So, here I was stuck and irritated. The doorbell rang, and before I even went to answer it, I already knew who it was. Bradley, my landlord, he never ceased to be on time when it came to collecting his rent. He was only twenty-five years old and owned most of the property here in Dallas. He was a more than often, well dressed, handsome, rich kid, who loved having the power that owning his properties gave him.

This was my second time being late on my rent in the last three months. I was sure he was going to evict me, that thought alone caused me to panic. I didn't know what I was going to do, as the doorbell rang again.

I stood up and exhaled. "Lord, please don't let this man kick me out of my home. You know, I'm trying to get it together. You've helped me overcome a lot. I need more time." I prayed looking at the ceiling.

I moved the curtain back from the window on the door. Sure enough, there was Bradley, standing on my porch with Ray-Ban sunglasses on, Chinos, and a button up blue Ralph Lauren shirt on. I shook my head and opened the door. Before I had the displeasure of inviting him inside, he strolled in wiping his feet on my Welcome Mat.

"Hey, Tasia, I don't mean to just drop by, but I was in the area, so I figured why not. He looked me up and down and bucked his eyes.

It wasn't until he did exactly that, that I thought about what I was wearing. Since I'd just waken up to check my PayPal account, I'd never changed out of my sleeping attire. I was wearing short gray boy shorts, and a tight tank top, without a bra. I could only imagine how much I was showing him. I figured I'd tell him, I didn't have his rent and rush him out of my home. Then I'd get in the shower and try to figure out what I was going to do to get the money for my rent. Maybe I could ask my father. He never really turned me down. Then I'd have to travel all the way to Houston just to spend the day with him. He was one of those types. He'd been trying to buy my love ever since I was a little girl.

"Wow, you look amazing. I always wondered what black girls looked like when they aren't all covered up," Bradley said, looking up and down my scantily clad body.

I frowned and covered my breasts with my arms. "Excuse you?"

"Oh, no, I'm sorry. I didn't mean anything by what I said. I'm sorry, I was kind of saying it to myself." He ran his fingers through his golden hair. "Okay, let's just cut to the chase. I noticed there wasn't any deposit made into your rent account. Is there a reason for that?" He asked trying to avoid looking over my body.

I pulled the crotch of my shorts out of my lips and straightened the leg holes all around my thigh. I hated how they kept on riding into my secret places. Bradley's eyes darted down to me, he blushed and turned red in the face. I could tell I was having an effect on him. He was carrying a tablet in his hand. I noticed him put it in front of his pants. That almost made me laugh out loud. Then it came to me, maybe I could use my charms against him. At least, so I could get an extension on my rent.

I walked over to the couch and bent over the arm of it. Fluffing one of the pillows. I made sure to spread my legs just enough, so my shorts would ride into my crack. I was blessed with a big apple bottom, I'd gotten from my mother. Mix that with my dark brown skin, D cupped breasts, and five-foot frame.

"Well, I was expecting some money from my daughter's father, but he stiffed me. So, now I'm going to have to figure something else out. Do you want to have a seat? Maybe I can get you a bottle of water or something." I looked over my shoulder at him.

He was staring right at my ass, I spread my legs further. He pulled at the flannel of his shirt. "But you promised me you'd be on time this month. Our agreement stated, if you weren't, I'd be forced to evict you. My hands are pretty much tied."

The word eviction made my heart skip a beat. I felt like I couldn't breathe. I stood up and faced him. "Wait, Bradley, you can't put me out on the street. I just moved in, I'm trying to get my life back on track after the Hurricane. Can't you just be a little patient with me? I'm really trying!"

He looked me up and down. "Well, I need my money, and you don't have that. So, what are you going to give me?" He looked into my eyes, then trailed his eyes all over my body.

I knew what he was thinking right away, and I wasn't going for it. I had never been with a white man before in my life. I had no desire to be with one. I was raised in a household where my father was a practicing Muslim, and Black Panther. My mother was a Panther as well. Both were from Oakland, California, and they were serious. They even felt some type of way about our mixed relatives. So, I could only imagine what they'd do and say if they knew how this white man was coming at me, and what I assumed he was proposing.

"Well, Bradley, if you can give me about a week. I can come up with the rent, maybe even pay you a little extra. Then next month I promise to be on time. We won't have this issue."

He smiled and shook his head. "Tomorrow is not promised to nobody, Tasia. Besides, I'm pretty sure we can work something else out. Hey, how about this, if you give me a lap dance, I'll wait the extra week, and you can pay me then. I'll act like you were never late. We'll let bygones be bygones. No harm no foul. What do you think?"

I stood there shocked. I couldn't believe this white boy actually had enough heart to ask me what he'd just asked. I didn't know what to say. But I knew I didn't want to be in the streets. I couldn't have my daughter trapping from one place to another like that. We'd just

experienced something mildly to that effect after Hurricane Harvey had touched down. I couldn't take her, nor
myself through that again. Dang, why did her father
have to be so trifling?

Bradley walked up to me and took a hold of my
hand. "Come on now, Tasia. With all this body that you
have, we could have worked out an arrangement a long
time ago. Black women are so fucking sexy, they drive
me nuts. You're blessed to have the finest race of
women on all of God's green earth. Now, how about
that dance, whatta ya say?" He stepped past me and sat
on the couch, placing his tablet on the table.

I stood there for almost two minutes in silence.
Could I possibly stoop so low, as to give in to this white
man's demands? Degrade me as a woman, and as a
mother of a seven-year-old little girl? Would I be able
to look myself in the mirror the next day? I didn't know.
What screamed louder than anything was the fact that I
had to make rent. I couldn't backtrack, I was more of a
woman than that. I took a deep breath and turned around
to face him.

"Okay, I'll give you a dance to one song. Then
we're through here. You'll give me a week to come up
with the money, and that'll be that. You got me?"

He smiled. "Honestly, I didn't hear a word you just
said. I was too busy staring at that chocolate camel toe.
God, you're so gorgeous."

I turned on *Ciara's 'Ride It'*, track, and made my
way over to him, feeling the butterflies in my stomach.

He held up a finger. "Wait a minute. I've been to
enough strip clubs to know how to get maximum pleasure from a dance." He unbuckled his belt, slid his pants
down to his ankles and patted his lap where he wore

nothing but a pair of silk underwear. Alright, let's go, Foxy Brown."

"My name is, Tasia. I ain't say nothing about no role-playing. Let's nip that in the bud, right now," I snapped, stepping in front of him, then turning around. I slow winded to the music and moved my body like a snake.

"Aw, yeah, would you look at that sexy black skin. Jesus Christ, now that's beauty." He grabbed me by the waist and pulled me back until I was sitting on his lap. I could feel his penis right under my butt, throbbing. To my surprise, it felt long and thick like I was sitting on a hot cucumber.

He placed his hands on my thighs. "Alright now, I know you feel what I'm working with. That's what I want you to dance on. Don't focus on nothing else. Come on baby," he hissed in my ear.

"My name is, Tasia, not baby." I felt his penis throb against me and I wanted to get up.

He wrapped his arms around my waist, trapping me, so I submitted. I slowly rotated my ass in a circular motion. Then rocked it back and forth, gripping his pole with my cheeks. I could feel it beat against my lips.

He opened his legs wider, and I fell into his lap all the way, smushing his penis. "Yeah, Tasia, that's what I'm talking about. You black Barbie. Aw, you feel so good, faster, Sexy Mama-faster," He growled and raised his hips from the couch, humping into me. His head pushed the material of my shorts into my sex lips.

"Calm down, Bradley. Now sit back and. let me do this," I gasped, moving back and forth on his dick. I hated that it was turning me on. I didn't like white boys.

I was only doing this for the rent. Once the song stopped, I would get up, I told myself.

He took a hold of my breasts and pulled me back to him. My nipples poked through the space between his finger. "Shut up, and just ride it. Aw, just like that black girl. Move that big booty in my lap." He pinched the sides of my shorts and yanked them upward, forcing the material into my ass crack turning them into a thong.

I moaned. The first thing I noticed was that it felt like I was sitting on hot skin. I moaned again and tried to look back at him. He held my waist and pulled downward causing me to squash his manhood. The song on the radio stopped, then repeated itself.

"Bradley, it stopped, our deal is complete. Let me go, now," I told him.

He sucked the back of my neck and sniffed my skin. "Just keep going and we can forget the rent. I'll credit you for the month." His hands went under my shirt, cupping my titties, squeezing them. He rose from the couch again and poked me with his dick.

I shook my head. "Uh-uh, I'ma just pay you. This has to stop, I'm not going there with you." I fought to free his arms from around me. But he held me too tight, all the while his hips continued to rise from the couch.

He pulled my nipples from their mounds, then pinched them. I shrieked and looked at the way his hands were moving under my shirt. Again, I hated myself for getting turned on. I wanted to get away from him.

"Okay, two months of rent. You don't have to pay me one red cent for two months. I swear I won't bother you, just let me suck these tits, please." He surprised me by picking me up and turning me around, so I was facing him. Manhandling my five-foot frame as if I were a rag doll. That caused the lips of my vagina to swell.

I hadn't even responded to him, yet he had my tank top pull up over my titties, sucking on the nipples one at a time. He pushed them together and nibbled on them, pulling them with his teeth. They stood from my breasts an inch a piece. He slobbered loudly over the surface of them.

"Aw, Bradley, please stop. Get off me, damn. Why are you so hard-headed?" I groaned but made no attempt to stop him from sucking my breasts. It felt so good, I felt all kinds of tingles shooting into my clitoris.

My essence ran out of me, and down my thighs, where his dick was out of the silk underwear and throbbing against me. The crotch of my boy shorts were drenched. I was praying he didn't notice that. He pulled my tank top all the way over my head and threw it to the carpet. My titties bounced out into the open. My nipples had never been harder. He licked the nipples, pushed my breasts up and licked under them. He even took his time to lick down my stomach where there were light stretch marks from when I had my daughter. They didn't seem to bother him at all. In fact, he traced his tongue along two of them.

"This chocolate tastes so good, it's so fucking good!"

I can't remember how it happened, but the next thing I knew, he had me balled up on the couch with my boy shorts hanging off my right ankle, while he licked up and down my slit. Sucking on each individual lip, before nipping at my clitoris, sending shivers through my entire body. I was screaming at the top of my lungs, creaming all over his lips.

"This black pussy. I love this black pussy!" Then more sucking, and licking. He held my labia all the way open and literally sucked my juices as they poured out of me, sending me to another climax that made me dizzy.

He stood up stroking his dick. "Come on, I'll knock off another month of rent. Come on, wrap those big pretty, perfect lips around my cock, and make me cum. Come on, Foxy!"

"It's Tasia, and I don't think so white man. I'll never suck your dick. I'm the daughter of Panthers," I said out of breath.

He gripped a handful of my hair and squeezed his dick with the other hand and rubbed his mushroom head across my lips. "Six months, Tasia. Six fucking months in all. Suck my cock, and I'll knock off six months. Please, just do it, already!" he groaned.

My mama and daddy was just gon' have to be mad at me. I opened my mouth and sucked his white penis in, grabbed it with my left hand and stroked it up and down, while I speared my head in his lap making loud sucking noises.

"Oh my, God! Oh my, God, Tasia! Tasia, aw this fucking black Goddess. You black fucking, Goddess. Aw-yes!" He humped into my mouth, fucking it as if it were a pussy, shivering, his knees threatened to buckle.

I slid my fingers into my box and worked them in and out of myself. I could only imagine what my parents would say if they found out. I imagined them walking into the living room while I was down on my knees like that and it made me pinch my clit. He pulled his dick out of my mouth creating a loud popping noise. My lips were still in an *'O'* shape ready to keep sucking. I could taste his precum on my tongue.

"A fucking year, I'm willing to forgo a fucking year. Just let me screw that black pussy between your legs. Let me stick this cock into that African gold mine," He said stroking his dick.

I don't know what had gotten into me. But, as bad as he wanted to stick his cock into my pussy, I wanted to feel it there just as much. Not to mention, to have a year off from paying rent was just an added incentive. I paid two thousand dollars a month, which meant that he was foregoing sixteen thousand dollars. I felt that my sex was worth it, so why not?

I bent over the table and felt him slap me on the ass. "This is my pussy tonight, Tasia. You're going to love this hard cock, I swear it." He smacked my ass again, then rubbed his piece up and down my slippery, wet slit, before pulling back and slamming it home in one thrust.

"Uhhh!" His white penis had finally penetrated my body. It felt like it traveled all the way into my stomach. He pulled it back, and slammed it back inside of me again, before picking up a steady pounding rhythm that had me screaming as if he were killing me. I was embarrassed by the sounds I made. As much as I hated to admit it, his shit felt so good. He hand soft warm hands explored my ass gave me everything he had to offer while my face slid across the top of the table. When I felt his thumb enter my asshole, I came so hard, screaming for him to fuck me harder.

"This my black pussy. It's mine-it's mine! You never have to pay rent again. Just give me this pussy!" He hollered, fucking me with every ounce of strength he had.

It took only a few minutes before he was cumming deep inside my channel. I could feel the squirts hitting my walls. That sent another wave of an orgasm through me. Bradley had made me cum seven times that night. Before it was all said and done, ya girl had secured a years' worth of rent.

I couldn't see myself giving him no more of this *black* pussy until rent rolled around again. But, by that time, I should be in a better position to handle shit myself. But who knows, thirty minutes of fucking to guarantee rent for the year, shit, what would you do?

Ca$h & Company

Breast is Best

I'd never felt more insecure about myself, then I did after I'd given birth to my only child, Seth. I went through a period where every time I came across a mirror, I refused to look in it from fear of what I would see staring back at me. Before my pregnancy, I weighed a consistent one hundred and forty pounds. After I gave birth to my son, I picked up about ten pounds of extra weight. Even though, I was five feet eight inches tall. It still made me feel pretty insecure because I was so used to being athletic, with a hard body. Now that I had a bit of a gut, I just didn't feel desirable.

On top of that, my breasts that were once a full C cup had blossomed to Double Ds. I was told since I was breastfeeding my son, my breasts were overproducing milk. So much so, that I had to pump them every hour or so. My son would have his fill, yet, I'd still be leaking, and aching like crazy. Then when I turned to my husband for relief he acted as if he was so turned off. I would turn to him in the hopes that he'd take delight in my breast milk, but all he'd do was grimace and turn me down.

In fact, ever since my son had been born my husband, Trevor and I's sex life has gone downhill. If I am lucky, we may do something about every three weeks. During those times, Trevor makes sure he stays away from my breast region and often proposes that I keep a shirt, and bra on during sex. It's so humiliating, I sometimes don't know what to think of myself.

Six months after Seth was born, Trevor's sister was emitted into the hospital and had to undergo a surgery on her back. During this time, Trevor thought it would be helpful if he took in her eighteen-year-old son, Malcolm for the three weeks it was going to take for her to have her surgery and recover. He asked me if I'd be okay with his nephew staying with us? I said that I didn't have a problem with it. For me, Malcolm had always been a very respectful, and kind young man. He was well mannered, and whenever he'd visit our home, he'd take it upon himself to help with the chores around the house as much as he could without me even asking him to.

Trevor was one of those men who felt like it was a woman's job to cook, clean and maintain the home. He rarely lifted finger to assist me with any tasks around the house. He said, his job was to pay the bills and bring food for the table. Everything else was my duty, and that was that. Well, it was so hard for me to keep up with everything around the house while having to care for a six-month-old child.

Trevor never seemed to pay our son any attention at all. So, while I was doing multiple chores around the house. I'd have to stop, care for and feed the baby, then rock him to sleep before going back to the endless tasks around our home. As soon as all of them were done, then it was time to cook and clean up after him. I swear I was so miserable, I felt like running away, and never coming back. Then again, whenever I saw my son's smile, all those thoughts would change at that moment.

Malcolm arrived at our home, one Sunday afternoon, right after we came home from church. When I opened the door, all five-feet-eleven inches of him stood in the doorway. He was caramel skinned, with two deep dimples in his cheeks, brown eyes, and was very muscular. He was a senior in high school, where he was scouted to play college football. He had this low haircut with deep ocean waves on top of his head.

He smiled and dropped his bag at his foot. "Monica, hey, how have you been?" He stepped inside and gave me a big hug, picking me up just a little bit and twirling me around, blowing my mind in the process.

As I've stated previously, I felt I was so overweight at this point that no man could get me off my feet without throwing his back out. But with one lift, Malcolm changed my mind. He placed me back on my feet and kissed my cheek. Then he took a step back, while still holding my hand. "Wow, you look absolutely amazing." His eyes trailed up and down my body.

Now I had known this boy ever since he was about fourteen years old. The entire time, I'd never looked at him as anything other than a child. But, his compliment had me feeling so good, I couldn't even explain it. "Thank you, Malcolm! You look good as well."

Trevor came from behind me and nudged me aside. "Watch out woman." He brushed past me and opened his arms wide, so he could give Malcolm a big hug. "Nephew, man, it's so good to see you. I got you all set up in the guest room. By the way, I heard what you just said to her. Please don't, that girl has gained a million pounds since, Seth. It's crazy here." He threw his arms around Malcolm's neck. "Come on, Kid. So, I hear you're being scouted by Notre Dame, Alabama, and LSU. Man, you're about to make it big time. Come and tell me all about it." Malcolm picked up his bag, he and I made eye contact, as he strolled past me with Trevor's arm around his neck.

I watched them disappear into the back of the house, to the guest room, that I had set up, not Trevor. My feelings were so hurt by Trevor's comments. I fell to my knees right there and broke down crying with my hands over my face.

* * *

The next morning started with an argument between, Trevor and me. It had been a rough night for, Seth. He'd spent most of the night crying his little heart out. So, that meant, I was back and forth from the nursery to our bedroom. At about six in the morning, Trevor decided he'd had enough. So, after going into the nursery to feed, Seth. When I got back to our bedroom door, I found it locked. I turned the knob over and over again in disbelief until I came to the realization I'd been locked out in the hallway, in just my nightgown. I beat on the door for what felt like forever, and instead of Trevor opening it, he yelled for me to go away, and kept it locked.

Malcolm opened the door to the guest room, rubbing his eyes. "What's the matter, Monica?" He stepped part way into the hall shirtless, in just his boxer briefs.

It looked as if he had an eight-pack of stomach muscles. His big thighs were perfectly sculpted with well-defined muscles in them. What really blew my mind was the imprint of his young penis pressed against his underwear. It looked like he was hiding a thick water hose down there.

When I noticed, I was staring I averted my eyes. "Oh, it's nothing, baby. Trevor's mad at me for running in and out of the room to the nursery, I guess I'll be sleeping on the couch for the rest of the morning. Go back to sleep." I turned to walk away.

He grabbed my hand. "Hey, you can take the guest room. I gotta get up anyway, so I can run my mile in the morning. It's really no problem."

I smiled. "No baby, I'm okay, but thanks for the offer. It was very kind of you." I made a move to walk away again, but I noted that he hadn't let my hand go. So, I turned back to face him.

Now his eyes were buck. He touched the front of my gown, right over the left nipple of my breast, and rubbed his fingers together. "Oh wow, I think you're lactating, look."

I glanced down at the front of my gown, and my face turned a bright shade of reddish caramel. Both of my nipples were oozing milk. The front of my gown was drenched. I was so embarrassed all I could do was cover them with my arms. "I'm sorry, Malcolm. I gotta go." I rushed into the bathroom and closed the door. I had never felt so dirty in all my life.

* * *

"I'm telling you, Malcolm. Whatever you do never get married, it sucks." Trevor said, picking up a bottle of beer and sipping out of it.

He and Malcolm were sitting in the living room watching Alabama versus LSU college football game on television. I'd just cooked them both a nice dinner and I guessed to cap it off they thought it would be cool to sit and watch some football. Seth was struggling from another ear infection, and I'd just given him his medication and put him to sleep. I was on my way back to our bedroom when I heard them talking.

"Nah, I don't know if I'm ready for marriage or anything like that. But, hey if I was, I'd most definitely have to get a beauty Queen like Monica, wow, she's everything. Am I right?" Malcolm asked.

Trevor sat the beer on the table and looked at him like he was crazy. "Are you kidding me. She gets on nerves my twenty-four seven. Always has that damn baby attached to her hip, and if that's not enough, she leaks more than a holey milk carton. I've never been more disgusted by a human being in all my life. Before the baby, aw man, she was so fine. Everywhere we went men couldn't help but stare at her. Women envied her, I felt proud to walk beside her. Now I make sure she walks either behind me or way up ahead."

Malcolm shook his head. "You're nuts, Unk. She's even more beautiful than the last time I saw her. I couldn't believe my eyes when she opened the door and I saw her for the first time after not seeing her in a while. I'd kill to be blessed with a wife like her when I get older."

Trevor laughed. "I'll tell you what, how about we switch places. I'll go off to college and smash every little hot piece of tail on campus, and you can stay here and drown in a marriage, with a woman whose best years are well behind her. My father always said that after a woman has a baby, it's a wrap, I should have listened." He took a hard swallow of his beer.

"You just don't know how wrong you are man, seriously," Malcolm said sitting back on the couch with a scowl on his handsome face.

I rushed into the bathroom, softly closed the door, and dropped to my knees after locking it. Tears poured out of my eyes, at the same time my breasts were lactating. I placed my forehead on the floor and broke all the way. down. I'd never felt uglier, or filthier than I did at that moment. The feeling got so intense that I thought about taking my life.

* * *

This same night, Trevor, rushed off to a poker game with four of his closest friends. He asked Malcolm if he wanted to go, but he declined saying he wanted to get a few hours of studying in. Trevor left, and Malcolm set up his laptop in the living room with his reading glasses on his face. I allowed him to study for about an hour before I stepped into the living room and asked him if he needed anything. Letting him know, I was about to turn in for the night since Seth had finally fallen asleep after a very active day of neediness.

He shook his head. "Naw, I'm good Monica, but thank you for asking. You have a good night's sleep. I'll see you in the morning." He smiled and went back to tapping away on his laptop.

"You too, baby." I left and went into my bedroom.

I knew I would not be able to get more than about three hours of sleep. Now that Trevor was gone, I was looking forward to getting some of the best sleep of my life. He was a restless sleeper and usually was all over the bed kicking and swinging his arm. I had to take advantage of his poker nights, which I did often. I was just pulling my nightgown above my waist, then the bedroom door opened, and Malcolm stepped inside the room catching me with both of my full breasts out in the open. I wrapped my arms around them. Them being folded against me like that, they began to leak. "Malcolm, what are you doing?"

He stepped further into the room and walked toward me. "I can't stop thinking about you. I don't like the way my uncle treats you. It's making me crazy." He stepped in front of me and held the sides of my arms. I could feel my milk sliding down my stomach. I felt so yucky.

"Malcolm thank you for feeling that way, but I'll be okay. Your uncle is who he is, I don't expect him to ever change."

He brushed my hair out of my face and looked into my eyes. "You deserve so much better than him. I wish I was old enough. I'd take you away, and treat you like the Queen you are. God if you only knew how beautiful you truly are." He leaned in and kissed my lips, running his hands all over my backside.

I was shocked and taken aback. I didn't know what to do. I knew it was so wrong, but at the same time, it felt so right. As long as, I didn't move my arms I would give him no reason to be disgusted by me. I only wanted to enjoy his demanding kiss. So, I sucked his lips and moaned hotly into his mouth.

He pushed me against the wall of the bedroom and moved my arms. "Let me see them. I've been dying to see them with the milk coming out." He held my arms at my sides, and shivered, before licking the liquid from my stomach. He cleaned it, then moved his lips up to my right nipple sucking on it just right, extracting the milk from my body. "You're beautiful! You're the most beautiful woman in the whole world. I'd trade places with my uncle in a heartbeat."

His compliments were driving me crazy. I needed to hear more of them. I needed to be restored. I'd been damaged for so long. His sucking noises were also driving me crazy. I placed my arms around his head, while he squeezed my breasts together, and sucked more of my milk. His Adam's apple moved up and down as he swallowed.

"Tell me more. How do my breasts look? Are they ugly, Malcolm, I need to know?"

He rubbed my hard nipples that were oozing all over his face coating it with my breasts milk. "I love them, they're perfect. I've never seen any more perfect than these. I swear to you." He sucked both nipples into his mouth at one time, while he held my boobies together, draining me. I was so turned on I snuck my hand into my panties, rubbing up and down my cat. It was dripping wet and aching.

Malcolm moved my hand out of the way and slipped one of his into my panties, separating my engorged lips, before putting a finger into my tunnel. "Ooh, you're so hot down there."

I stood on my tippy toes and cocked my head back, pressing my breasts against his chest. "Tell me, I'm beautiful, Malcolm. I need to hear that some more," I said out of breath, as his finger went in and out of me at full speed.

He added another one and kept going. "You're so fine, Monica. You're a pure dime. I'd marry you in this life, and the next ten if I could. I'm super jealous of my uncle. And I hate him because of you. I swear to God I mean that." He grabbed my right breast, and squeezed it, sucking the leaking nipple back into his mouth, swallowing my contents.

I humped forward and back on his two invading digits. His words playing over and over in my head, sending me on a journey all on their own. "Uh, it feels so good! I'm so wet. Can you feel that?" I huffed and puffed.

He picked me up and sat me on the bed. Right on top of Trevor's uniform, he'd taken off that evening after work. He spread my thighs, and stuck his face between them, while his big hands massaged my boobies. Milk ran in between his fingers and dripped off his wrist. I pulled my panties to the side. I was tired of him licking me through the cotton, I needed to feel his heat on my most sensitive areas down there. I'd been neglected for so long, that it felt good to be wanted, to be desired by such a handsome young man, who I felt could of had any woman he wanted in this world. But there he was choosing me. I felt special, and like to hell with, Trevor.

Malcolm ate me out like he was an expert. He held my lips apart, and trapped my clit with his lips, running his tongue in circles around it over and over again. I was making so much noise, I feared I would wake up, Seth. I had to grab a pillow off the bed and scream into it. He ran three fingers in and out of me. "Cum for, cum for me. I need to taste you. You're so fine! I need to taste you, please cum," He growled, giving me more of his assaults.

I rose from the bed, opened my thighs wide, squeezed my breasts together, and started to cum all over his mouth While he fingered me like an animal. I was shaking so bad my teeth were chattering. He climbed up my body, and got between my legs, already nude from the waist down, took his rock-hard penis, popped the head into my tight hole, and slammed it home. I hollered and came all over again. Then he was making love to me like a complete monster, licking all over my boobs, sucking the milk from them, and off the surface of my stomach, and chest.

His eyes rolled backward. "I knew it. I knew it, I knew it would be this good! Geez, please touch me," He groaned, pounding in and out of me with so much force, he was hitting my G-spot every single time.

I hadn't gotten the opportunity to see his manhood, but from the feel of it, I knew it was huge. My tunnel was completely filled up. I rubbed all over his eight-pack abs, and squeezed his young chest, with their hard nipples. I dug my nails into his back as his penis beat away at my walls. I couldn't help cumming again. This caused more milk to shoot out of my nipples. He sucked it up immediately, sending me into another orgasm.

"From the back, Monica. Let me hit this from the back. I want to see your pretty boobs rock back and forth, while I hit this from the back."

As soon as I got into the position, I could hear him groan behind me. He ran his hand all over my backside, opened the cheeks and licked in between them, then sucked on the ring to my anus, before getting behind me, and sliding into my sex from the back. From this angle, I could feel all of him. He took a hold of my breasts and started to really go to town on me, harder than before.

"Aw, Monica, it's so good. It's so good! My uncle stupid, I can't take it. I can't take it, I'm cumming already," He moaned, speeding up the pace, and long stroking like I've never been stroked before.

He growled, then his cum was shooting into me. At the same time, his fingers pinched my nipples causing milk to skeet out of them. After he released his passions into my body, he pulled out of me, still at full attention.

His piece throbbed in the air, fully engorged. "You see what you do to me. This is how sexy you are. I'll never get tired of this body. You are perfect. No man can do what you can do with this body, you create life. If it takes all night, I'm gon' get that through your head. Come here, baby." He pulled me to him.

Tears rolled down my cheeks, as we embraced. I could feel the length of him throbbing against my stomach. "Thank you so much, Malcolm. You have no idea what that means to me." I grabbed ahold of his pipe that was so long and thick, I was surprised it had been able to go inside of me. Let me show you how much I appreciate you."

It's been four months now, and Malcolm and I continue to get together every weekend to make love. I've never felt so blessed to have him in my life. I've done everything in my power not to become emotionally attached, but when you have a gorgeous young man like him, that is not only giving you multiple orgasms with every sex romp but also feeding the emptiness inside of you, it is so hard. For now, I'll continue to enjoy what we have while I build up my courage to leave Trevor's trifling ass behind. I deserve better. Malcolm's right, I can produce life. There should be a daily celebration of me because I am a woman.

Big Girls Need Love Too

"Girl, I'm telling you, when I hit this club, and these niggas see me in this three-thousand-dollar purple Prada dress, they gon' break their necks to talk to me, watch," Tyra said, looking into my full-length mirror over her shoulder at her ass.

I had to admit it was perfect. I sat there on the edge of my bed wishing I could've been as fine as her with her light skin, green eyes, and long silky hair that fell down a slender back, attached to a figure that would rival any top-notch stripper. She was something to see, I didn't have to have a penis to admit that.

I exhaled loudly, as I clutched my Prada dress to my chest. I doubted if mine would look even a pinch as good as hers would while it was draped across my frame. I felt so insecure sitting there looking at her. While Tyra was about five-feet-five-inches tall, with a nice tight body, small breasts, and a big booty.

I was the same height but weighed about thirty pounds more than she did. I had a nice amount of stomach that got most of the attention when I wore tight dresses or shirts.

My thighs were too big to me, and if my dress rose high enough a person would be able to make out the cellulite decorated all over the backs of them. My face was a bit pudgy and always had been ever since I was a little girl. I wasn't the girl that got the, *"Ohhh, she's so beautiful"*, or, *"Wow, she's pretty."* No, I was the girl that got the long pauses, then the, *"You can tell she's healthy,"* and the, *"You gotta stop feeding that girl or she'll blow."*

Even as an adult, for me, the compliments were few and far in between. I wasn't given any attention. Even when I went above and beyond to have my hair, and nails hooked up. I dressed nicely, and always smelled good. I was polite, and complimented others as much as I could, hoping I'd receive some form of a compliment in return, but nothing. It never happened, life was shitty.

Tyra ran her hands over her flat stomach and smiled in the mirror. She'd had two kids, ate what she wanted, and still looked as if she couldn't gain a single pound. As much as I loved her, part of me envied her to the point of disdain.

"Girl, you better get yo' butt up and get dressed! We gotta be there in an hour. You know it's gone take you at least that to get all your parts in order." She laughed and turned back to the mirror. "Shid, I ain't got, time for your sulking tonight. My kids with the babysitter and I look good, I'm ready to turn up. You better have a snack a something. That always cheers you up."

Oh yeah, and that was another thing. Tyra had a habit of teasing me about my weight. She did it when we were alone. Not in front of other people. I don't think she honestly knew how much her comments affected my self-esteem. I'd tried my best to tell her once, but she blew it off as me being emotional. So, I never tried again, because I left feeling worse than I had before.

"Dawn, did you hear me? Get yo' big butt up and let's go," she demanded.

I'm so tired of this skinny bitch.

* * *

Ten minutes later, while Tyra was in the bathroom talking on her cell phone. I locked the door to my bedroom and stood in front of the full-length mirror with misty eyes, especially after seeing how Tyra looked standing in front of it. I grabbed two handfuls of my big stomach, and held them, dropped it and watched them bounce. Then I turned around to look at my booty, with the thong between the cheeks. I ain't have no problem there, that backside was nice. I didn't care what nobody said. At least I liked my ass. I wished I could fall in love with the rest of my body. I looked down the back of my legs, then turned back around and held up my stomach, so I could see the stretch marks around my waist.

"Why couldn't you make me beautiful, Father? Why do I have to go through life as an ugly duckling? It's just not fair!" I grabbed the dress off the bed and continued the process of making myself as beautiful as I could.

* * *

In the car, Tyra, couldn't sit still in the passenger's seat. "It's a change of plans girl. Do you remember that dude, Hines, that we went to school with back in the day? You know he was Asian and Black? And always dressed real fresh. He was supposed to be drafted to the NFL after one year of college." She asked flipping down the visor to check her make up in the mirror.

"Yeah, what about him?" I asked, turning into what looked like a traffic jam. I looked over my shoulder to see if I could make a U-turn to get up out of there. Sometimes I really hated the traffic in Denver.

"Well, he just hit me up. He invited us to his private room, well he invited me, and a plus one. I was going to bring my sister, but screw that. That bitch is just as bad. I can't be competing for his attention. I need all eyes on me. You're perfect." She giggled and ran lip gloss over her cherry red lips.

I felt like she'd just punched me in the gut. I felt so sick, I could have thrown up in her lap, and maybe I should have. "Yeah, well, I'm glad I can be of some assistance to you. Thanks for bringing me along." I rolled my eyes and made the U-turn successfully. "Type his address into the GPS, so I can get us there with your conceited ass. Ugh!"

After punching in the address, Tyra sat back and exhaled. "You think I'm conceited though?"

"I think you're vain as ever, but it's cool. You're a very beautiful female. You have the right to feel how you feel. I just wish you were a little nicer towards me sometimes, but other than that, you're good." I laid my hand on her thighs and shook it to let her know I was okay.

"Hey, I'm sorry, Dawn. You know I don't mean to come down so hard on you. I just be feeling myself. It's like you gotta be this fine to understand. But, it's somebody out there for everybody. At least that's what my mother always told my half-sister. She fat as hell, too, so maybe my mother was just throwing her a bone, or a ray of hope." She shrugged her shoulders. "I don't know." She rummaged through her knock-off Prada bag and pulled out a Snickers bar. "Want a piece? I ain't ate shit all day." She gave me a look that said she hoped I said no, and I did.

Cum For Me 4

* * *

Hines had a private room at the Sybaris Pool Suites. It was a real nice setup, with a waterfall inside the room that had a curved slide connected to the pool. There was a fireplace inside it as well, as a Jacuzzi and two big beds. He opened the door with a white Gucci robe on that was open enough for me to see he wasn't wearing a shirt underneath. His abs were popping, and his chest was well defined. I could see the hint of his nipples, I had to admit he had me feeling some type of way. I was trying to drink in as much of him as possible, so I could have his visual in my mind when I had solo time that night, or in the morning. I'd needed some form of release after seeing this specimen of a man.

Tyra stepped up to him and kissed him on the cheek. "Hey baby, you gone let us in, or are we gon' stay in this hallway all night?" She asked with her bottom lip poked out.

He laughed and hugged her. "Of course, you can come in. It's the reason I called you over here." He kissed her cheek and allowed her to pass by him. "There is Moet in the bucket of ice over there. Help yourself." He turned back and looked down on me. "And who do we have here? Don't tell me this is, Dawn Robinson, from John Elway high school? The leader of the dance team, and class valedictorian?" He held his arms opened.

My eyes were open so big, I was afraid my forehead was going to have stretch marks on them when they finally closed.

"How in the hell do you remember all of that? I don't even know your last name or anything about you." I said neglecting to step into his arms.

Even though he was handsome, I didn't know him like that. Yeah, I would use his image in private, and in fantasy, but that had nothing to do with our reality.

He laughed. "Wow, that was a shot at me I guess." he nodded. "Well, you were a year older than me. But I watched you closely, and I've always had a major crush on you. Whenever the dance team used to dance at our rallies. I could never take my eyes off you. You had the most coordination, and you just made everything look good. It's an honor to meet you as an adult." He held his arms open again.

"Can I have a hug?"

I stood there for a second, wondering if I was being pranked. How could this fine man have remembered all that about me? I was wondering if Tyra had put him up to this. Are you jerking my chain?" I asked stepping into his arms, smelling his cologne that cast a spell on me.

I wrapped my arms around his lower waist. His bare chest rubbed against my chubby cheek. He felt hot, and his body was solid like he was made of steel. Jesus Christ, now this was a man.

He laughed. "Nah, I wouldn't play games like that. Life is too short, and I'm way to busy. I remember being terrified to talk to you, so I never did. It's probably why you don't remember me. But, it's still crazy because damn near every female from our high school done hit me up on Facebook trying to see what's good after I got drafted in the first round into the NFL. Never got a friend request from you though."

Tyra appeared in the doorway with a bottle of Moet in her hand. "Dang, Hines quit playing wit' my friend and let her in. I'm trying to get acquainted with you." She stood on her tippy toes and sucked his earlobe into her mouth.

He nodded at her and looked back down on me. "I want to talk to you a little more before the night is out. I got a lil' more courage now that, I am a man. I ain't afraid as I used to be." He winked at me and stepped aside.

* * *

An hour later, and after three glasses of champagne, I was ready to head home, so I could get some rest. I was tired, and all I could think about was my bed, and the pillow laying on it. Tyra was all over, Hines, so much I wasn't sure if he was able to breathe. They sat on the couch across from me, with her straddling him. Her short Prada dress was along her waist. Her thong was visible to my eyes I watched her slide her hand between her legs and rubbed her kitten through her panties.

"Umm, Hines. Why don't you let me get some of this pipe I've heard so much about? I know you want me, stop fronting like you don't." She bit into his neck, causing him to close his eyes.

When they opened, they were looking over at me. She slapped him across the face. Then looked over her shoulder at me. "Who, Dawn? Yeah, right, stop playing, and let me get some of this." She rubbed her hands all over his perfect athletic body. She sucked his neck again, leaned back and pulled her shoulder straps down her arms, exposing her supple breasts that were about a firm C cup. "You wanna touch 'em?"

He shook his head. "I've had females like you swarming all over me my whole life. There is nothing special about you. But, Dawn, Dawn is a Diamond." He shook her off him, and slid across the short distance, onto the couch beside me. "How you doing over here, Baby girl? Can I keep you company?"

Tyra looked across the room at us with her eyes wide open. She was stunned. Her titties were out in the open. Her dress was pulled around her waist. Seeing her in that state caused my pussy to become wet, my panties were soaking.

I looked into his eyes and trembled. "Why would you prefer to spend your time with me, instead of her? She's ten times badder than I am. I'm just her friend. I gotta get home anyway."

He kneeled in front of me, with his hands on my knee. "Not before I get to taste of you. You've been my fantasy girl ever since I was a horny little boy. I gotta see what this taste like." He pulled my skirt all the way up and cocked my legs wide open.

"Are you fucking kidding me. You're going to choose my fat ass friend, over me! Yeah, the fuck, right, Hines!" Tyra snapped.

He ignored her and stuck his face all the way between my thighs and kissed the crotch of my panties, then licked up and down them. He slowly removed my thongs from my body and dropped them on the carpet beside us. "Just let me prove how I feel about you."

The next thing I knew he was licking up and down my crease, sucking over my lips as if they were oysters on a half shell. I started to moaning and humping his face. Still, in disbelief, he'd chosen me instead of my fine ass friend. But, as I looked over at her sour face, glaring at us, I knew it was the truth, and it made the moment that much more special to me.

"Yes, Hines, it feels lovely baby. Damn, Tyra, you don't know what you're missing." I teased, looking over at her with my eyes lowered into slits. He started to attack my clit, sending shivers up and down my spine.

"You smell so good, I knew you would. Aww, baby, you taste so good." He turned me over and had me hold the back of the couch with my ass in the air. His tongue traveled up and down my slit, stopping on the crinkle of my backdoor before he stabbed it over and over again. I could hear him slobbering all over me. His thumb ran circles around my clitoris. I bucked and screamed with my head tilted toward the ceiling as my orgasm ripped through me.

"Aw-shit, Tyra! I'm cumming, girl he got my *fat ass* cumming!" I hollered, shaking out of my mind.

Hines continued to suck me into oblivion until I came, twice all over his mouth. He sat back on his haunches with my juices dripping off his chin. His face looked like he'd used to much baby oil, but I knew it was all my essences on his cheeks. He stood up and dropped his robe to the floor. His big dick stood out like a flagpole. He stroked it, rubbing my booty, slid two fingers inside of me, and pulled them out, sucking them into his mouth, hungrily.

Tyra rushed to his side and fell to her knees. She yanked his dick out of his hand, sucked it into her mouth, and deep throated him.

Then she popped it out loudly. "Just fuck me first, then. I don't care if you do her, too. But I want you first, you know this bitch can't fuck with my bidness. Look at her!" she snapped.

I stood up, walked around her thirsty ass and grabbed his hand. "Come on, baby, show this bitch what she ain't finna get none of," I said looking him in the eyes, leading him to the big bed alongside the waterfall that splashed into the pool.

He nudged her aside and rushed to pick me up. "Put me in this pussy, Dawn. All I want is you, I ain't thinking about, her. Do it, baby, let's fuck!"

I wrapped my legs around him, stunned that he was able to lift me in the air like I was as light as a feather. I trembled in his big arms, went behind myself, found his penis and pushed it into my hole that was pouring out my love juices.

His hardness sank into me, I yelped and dug my nails into his shoulders. "Awe, Hines! Do me, baby! Do me—" I whimpered.

He tossed me up and down, thrusting inside of my body, juicing me. His tongue roamed all over my neck and chin. then his teeth were in my neck. He growled while fucking me like a champion. Tyra sat on the couch with her hand between her legs and her dress pulled up to her stomach, working her fingers in and out of herself. Her eyes were trained on Hine's penis shooting in and out of me. His log traveled to the deepest region of my womb, over and over again.

He laid me back on the bed and pulled me to him, slamming his cock in and out of me. He was tearing my pussy up, it felt like he was so deep, I could barely breathe.

Sweat dripped off his face. "Uh-uh-uh-uh, Dawn, I awe shit, baby. Aw shit, you're so perfect. You're so perfect!" He hollered digging into me faster.

I closed my eyes, as they rolled into the back of my head. When I came, I rose to an upright position while he pounded away and bit his chest. Then fell back on the bed and moaned as loud as I could. I'd never been dicked down the way that he was dicking me. He rubbed all over my stomach, and up and down my thighs. It seemed like the more he touched me, the harder his piece became until it got so long, I tried to back away from him.

His dick slipped out of me. I nearly made it off the bed, when he grabbed my ankle and pulled me back to him. He jumped on top of me, forced my right knee to my ribs, and forced his big cock back inside of me. He sucked on my neck and proceeded to do me right, while his teeth locked into the back of my neck. His growling had me cumming back to back.

Tyra came over and jumped in the bed beside us, dropped her head to our sexing crotches, and licked both of them. She shocked the hell out of me, because as long as we'd been friends. I'd never seen, nor heard of her doing anything like that.

"Do me, now, Hines! She's had enough. Do me like you doing her," She groaned, I could feel her lip brush against my pussy while his dick pushed in and out of me.

"No, no. It's all about, her. This my pussy! This my pussy, now. Aw shit, I'm cumming, Dawn, I'm cumming!" He slammed into me and released his seed deep in my belly.

His cream splashed against my walls so hard I could feel it. That sent me into oblivion. I couldn't believe that a man as fine as him could actually cum from a woman of my likes. It drove me crazy. I bounced my ass back into his lap forcing more of his nut out of him until he was spent. He pulled out of me and opened my ass, licking up and down it. His tongue played magical tricks on my anus before he sucked all over my body, and each individual toe. Tyra never did get a chance to get any of him that night.

Exactly two months later, he became my husband, and we've been married for ten years strong. Before Hines came into the picture, I never thought a man could actually love me enough to appreciate me for me. But, then, God sent me him, with my husband I can be myself. He's taught me how to love myself. I just want all of you ladies to know that men love us, too. You ain't gotta be some lil' boney female in order to land your Knight in shining armor. Your one is out there. Just keep loving yourself and remain in prayer. The Lord knows big girls need love, too.

Force Me

I was running around the house like a chicken wit' its head cut off, trying to get everything in order before my father arrived. I had not seen him in person, in nearly two years. Between the stresses of life, the eighty-plus hour work weeks, all while studying to become an Architect, it was so hard to find time for the close relationship I'd once shared with my father.

My mother passed away when I was only three years old, leaving my father as an only parent. I had been my mother and father's only child. For the next seven years, it had just been me and my father, Carl. In my opinion, he had done a very good job of raising me and trying his best to fill the void my precious mother left behind. We developed an unbreakable bond and continued to share one even to this day. My father didn't remarry until I was eighteen years old, and off to college. I'm not even sure if he dated until I left the house completely. If he had, I never met any of his women or heard anything about him being involved with anyone. He did all that he could to ensure, that I lived a normal drama free life. I appreciated him for that.

My father moved away from our hometown of Chicago, Illinois, only a few months back to a small city in Wisconsin, that I had never heard of before. Him moving made things very hard for me because for so long he had been my everything. I was used to us eating breakfast every morning together. We jogged in the afternoons together and had dinner every other night together. When I say my dad was my everything, I mean that. So, when he moved away to a small city called

Madison, it left me vulnerable and devastated. When he agreed to finally come visit me, I couldn't have been more excited than a child's first visit to *Toys R' Us*.

I finished getting the house up to par as best as I possibly could. I had everything nice, neat, and organized with some fresh incense burning and a nice amount of Febreze in the air. Just like me, my father was big on scents. I couldn't wait to see him, I had so many things planned for us to do. He was supposed to be here for two days and my planner was booked. I wanted to make sure he enjoyed every single hour with me. Boy, I couldn't wait, it had been so long since we'd been on a father and daughter date. I didn't care how old a girl got, she always needed her father. The bond between a father and daughter is priceless. It meant the world to me at least.

Imagine my face when I opened the door only to find my father standing in front of it, with his arm wrapped around a female who looked to be my age of nineteen, or maybe a few years older. My jaw dropped, I wanted to know who she was asap.

"Hey, Baby Girl," He exclaimed, opening his arms wide, stepping into the house to hug me.

He picked me up off my feet and twirled me around in the living room. My father, Carl, stood six feet two inches tall, with a bald head, and was very muscular. He was a former personal trainer and retired Fire Fighter, who'd always been physically fit. So, lifting my five foot four inches, one-hundred-twenty-pound body into the air was no task for him. Even as irritated as I was by the presence of this female on his arm, I couldn't help laughing like I was a little girl again.

"I'm okay, Daddy! I've missed you so much," I said hugging his neck.

He placed me back on my feet and kissed my forehead, making me melt. I had really missed that. He took a step back then grabbed the female's hand. "Baby, this is Shondra, she's my Fiancée." He stepped behind her, wrapped his arms around her waist and kissed the side of her neck.

Shondra extended her hand. "How are you doing, Lisa? I've heard nothing but great things about you. It's a pleasure to finally meet you."

Instead of shaking her hand, I looked her up and down in horror. As she stood there with her light skin and green eyes. Dressed in a tight Burberry dress that clung to every curve on her body and trust me there were a lot of them. She also had a French Manicure and matching pedicure. She was so pretty, that was a fact, I couldn't lie about, I got jealous. I was wondering how long it was going to be before she stole my father away from me completely. I felt like bursting into tears.

"Uh, may I ask how old you are to be dating, or should I say, engaged to my father?" I crossed my arms in front of me and looked her up and down ready to put a Chiraq beat down on her ass.

She exhaled and looked back at my father. "I told you this was going to be a problem, Carl." She turned her back on me and stepped behind him, that really pissed me off. It was like she was using my father for protection against me. I'm his Baby girl, not her that made me so angry tears welled up in the corners of my eyes. I felt my heart breaking.

"Lisa, can we please go somewhere and talk?" My father asked looking down on me.

He reached to touch my chin, but I jerked away from him. Something I'd never done before in all my life. "Yeah, because this is just ridiculous. I thought we were going to spend this weekend together." I stormed down the hallway headed toward my bedroom, with tears running down my cheeks.

My father stepped into the room and closed the door behind him. "Now, that was completely uncalled for, Lisa. You haven't even given Shondra a chance. That's not right."

I turned around to face him. "What not right, is that you show up to my doorstep with this woman, I've never heard of until a few moments ago. Then to find out you're engaged. Wow!" I held up my hands signaling that my mind was blown. I didn't know what to do, I was so angry. "How old is she dad?"

My father lowered his head and sighed. "She's twenty-two, but very mature for her age. If you give her a chance you will find that to be true. Now come back in here and behave like a grown woman instead of a child."

I scoffed. "Twenty-two years old! I'm not the only child in this house, right now. That's for sure."

He grabbed my wrist and smacked me hard on my butt. "Now that's enough. You're going to finish getting dressed, and we're going to go out and have a gay ol' time. I'll see you in front of this house in ten minutes. Get yourself together."

I waited for him to close the door before I rubbed my butt where he'd slapped it. I felt like breaking down all over again. Not only were these new developments sprung on me, but my father was acting like I had no right to feel how I was feeling. I think that's what hurt me the most.

* * *

Like a good girl, I took my time and got dressed, still thinking about Shondra the whole time. I made sure to put on a number that would crush the Burberry dress she was wearing. I chose a nice red and black Fendi dress, that clung to my every curve. I fixed my natural curls so that they fell around my shoulders. Then called my God-Father, Savon. Savon and my father had been best friends for thirty years. My parents had even named him as my God-Father. But, a few months back, Savon, and my father had a falling out over one of their many businesses they had together going under. Each man blamed the other one. Long story short, they haven't spoken to each other since that night.

When I came out into the living room, Savon was already there. He stood six-foot-three-inches tall, was as muscular as my father because he played in the NFL for ten years and had done a great job maintaining his physique. He was also bald like my dad with a nice well-trimmed goatee, that had specks of gray in it. All my friends swore up and down that he was the most handsome older man they'd ever seen, and as much as I hated to admit it, so did I. The reason I'd invited him out with us was because I didn't want to be alone with my father and his new young fiancée that was only a few years older than me. Plus, I wanted to make my father jealous, because Savon had never neglected to treat me like a Princess. He'd been that way ever since I was a little girl.

When I stepped into the living room, I could tell things were kind of tense, and that made me happy. My father stood with his arm around Shondra and a scowl on his face. Shondra looked me up and down and bucked her eyes. Obviously, shocked by my transformation. I didn't want her thinking she'd be the only bad bitch in the room. That wasn't happening.

"Wow, you look amazing, Lisa. I'm serious," She said nodding her head.

"Thank you," I returned pulling my dress down just a bit. It kept riding up on my butt with every step I took.

Savon smiled and walked over to me, wrapping me in his embrace. "Hey, Baby girl. You look absolutely, stunning. Thank you for calling me out tonight." He hugged me tighter and dared to kiss me on the neck.

His lips lingered on my skin before he rubbed his hands down my back and looked into my face.

* * *

I couldn't enjoy my meal at the expensive restaurant because Shondra acted like she had to feed my father every bit of his steak. Then she would wipe his mouth with the napkin like he was a little kid. They kissed way too much, and nobody could get a word in edgewise, because her mouth kept running like a faucet. Ugh, I was so annoyed and ready to pounce on her ass. I guess Savon sensed that because he placed his big hand on my thigh under the table to calm me down. I was so thankful he did because I was ready to go haywire.

Midway through the meal, Shondra looked across the table at me and held up her glass of Champagne. "To new beginnings and eternal relationships. May we all find our places in life and learn how to stay in them. Here, here," She held the glass over my plate and looked me in the eyes challenging like.

I picked up my glass ready to throw the contents in her face, when I felt Savon, squeeze my thigh under the table then slide his hand under the hem of my dress along my inner thigh. His knuckles rested against my panties. I looked over at him and he shook his head.

"Just toast her, Baby Girl. Let's make this a good evening." He ran his finger up and down my crease.

I was so shocked because he had never done anything like that before. I was wondering if maybe it was his way of calming me down because he knew how explosive my temper could get. He'd always told me I had a temper like my mother.

Before I could tap my glass against hers my father did it with his. "It's okay, baby. I got you, I'm not gon' let your toast go to waste. Come here." He tilted her chin toward him, and right there in front of me and Savon, they tongued each other down like they were in a bedroom. Her hand disappeared under the table and I could only imagine what she did with it.

Me, personally, I'd had enough. I jumped up and scooted back from the table. "Savon, take me home. I can't deal with this bull crap no more. I've had enough."

"Lisa, sit down and let's finish this meal," My father ordered.

"I don't know, Daddy, she looks pretty pissed. Maybe she should go," Shondra urged wrapping her arm around his neck and kissing his cheek.

"Daddy? Bitch, he's not your, Daddy, he's mine! Go find your own," I snapped ready to rush around the table.

Savon grabbed me. "Baby Girl, it's okay. I'll take you home. Carl, Shondra, I guess she'll see you guys later." He tossed four fifty dollar bills on to the table. "It was nice meeting you, Shondra. I wish you two all the best."

"But Lisa, wait—" My father began, but it was too late. I was already out the door of the restaurant and headed toward Savon's Jaguar.

* * *

I kicked off my red bottoms as soon as I came through the door of my home, then stopped and rubbed my temples. "Thank you for bringing me home, Savon. I'm sorry   I ruined our evening," I said over my shoulder getting ready to close the door knowing he would leave right away as usual. Before I could turn all the way around to close and lock it, Savon wrapped his arms around me and lead me up against the wall face first.

He started kissing and biting all over my neck. His front humped into my bottom. "You need, Daddy to-night, don't you, Baby Girl?" He yanked my dress up around my waist.

"No, get off me, I just wanna be alone." I pushed back into him to free his hold as my heart pounded in my chest.

"You wanna be the only, Baby Girl, that's all that is. I know what you need." He pulled my thongs to the side, and kneeled behind me, then started sucking all over the backs of my thighs.

His tongue trailed all the way up until he sucked my juices through my panties. His big hands rubbed all over my booty, opening it before his tongue invaded my hole. "You're my, Baby Girl, too. I told you, anything he won't do, I'll do for you. I'm Daddy!"

"Stop, get off me Savon, you're supposed to be my God-Father. This ain't right." I wiggled out of his grasp then ran with my thongs around my thighs and dress up to my stomach.

I could feel my juices running down my legs. I couldn't believe Savon would come at me like this. I was about twenty feet away from my bedroom door. I knew if I could get in there, I could lock it and maybe he'd stop and think about what he was trying to do to his God-Daughter. I would have blamed it on the alcohol. But, before I could get there, he tackled me to the floor. I landed on my stomach.

He pushed my knees to my chest and began devouring my kitty from the back. "You're my, Baby Girl. You're mine just as much as you are his." His tongue ran up and down my crease. He nipped at my clitoris and slurped my juices as they poured out of me.

I tried to get up, but the feeling he was giving my body made me so weak. It lowered my ability to resist. Once again, I was in shock, I couldn't believe Savon. The first wave of my orgasm rocked my body. I screamed and opened my thighs wide. Then I held my right knee in the air while he sucked and slid his tongue in and out of my box.

I tried to get up again. "Stop, Savon, this ain't right, it's not right. I'm your God-Daughter." I jumped up and pushed the door to my room on wobbly legs. I walked backward until the bed hit the back of my knees, and I fell on it.

Savon pulled his shirt over his head, revealing a rock-hard body. His fraternity symbol was branded on his left ear. I could see his penis sticking up against his pants. The indentation looked huge. "Come here, Baby Girl. I got you, you know I do."

I shook my head. "I ain't going. This ain't right and you know it." I stood up and pulled my dress all the way down. I could feel my nipples sticking through it. My panties were drenched, they were wetter than they'd ever been before.

Savon rushed me, picked me up and threw me on the bed. He pulled my dress up and my panties down off my body. His hand went between my thighs, rubbing all over my wet and bald kitty.

"Give me some of this, Baby Girl. Let Daddy make you feel all better." He sucked my hard nipple through my dress and opened my pussy lips, rolling his thumb all around the clitoris.

When his lips landed on top of mine, his tongue shot into my mouth, then he held my bottom lip with his teeth.

I opened my legs wider and yanked my head backward. "I'm yo', Baby Girl, huh? So, I guess you want me to do this then?" I unbuckled his pants and pulled his eleven-inch monster out. I stroked it up and down, before sucking the huge head into my mouth. I started sucking it as best I could while he rubbed all over my ass and fingered me.

We wound up in a 69 position, with me seated right over his face, riding his tongue slowly. I couldn't help moaning all over his big tool. "This ain't right, Daddy. We're so wrong. Aww, my God. What are you doing down there? Un!" I moaned sucking on his head.

It was as big as a crab apple. I knew I was wrong for doing what I was, but all I could see was my father and his new lady friend all over each other. That made me want to lash out, and what better way than the way I was doing it? Besides, Savon was working magic on my little kitty, like a grown ass man, who was far from a rookie.

He opened my pussy lips wide, and tongue fucked as he pinched my clit. It felt so good all I could do was hold his dick in my hand, while I rode his face with my head tilted toward the ceiling.

"Daddy, Daddy, aww yes! Force me. Make me cum! Shit!" My whole body began to shake. I screamed, cumming as hard as I could.

Savon didn't let up. He continued to savor my pearl as my body convulsed. He laid me on my stomach and swiped his tongue across my ass cheeks. "This is how a man is supposed to appreciate his Baby Girl. Damn, girl. I couldn't take my eyes off you in this dress tonight. I had to have you." He opened my cheeks and sucked my anal ring into his mouth, went back to my ass then pulled me to my knees. "It's Daddy time, baby." He pumped his dick and grabbed a fistful of my hair. He slowly guided himself into my box from the back stretching me open.

My jaw dropped, my eyes closed tight, and I spread my knees. "Yes, Daddy! Come on, force me to take that dick. Force me!" I hollered, slamming back on him to impale myself on his monster.

He gripped my hips, working his dick in and out of me. "Baby girl—baby girl! Uh-uh, you so thick. You so thick, uh-damn. Damn, baby, it barely fit-it barely fit!" He smashed forward even harder.

I rocked back and forward, feeling him sawing in and out of my sex. Every time I slammed backward, I could feel him burrowing into my stomach. Then it was gone again, only to go deeper. My eyes rolled in the back of my head. I couldn't believe my father's best friend was fucking me. My God-Father, the man that had always been there for me when my father was unable to be. I never thought he'd even noticed me in that light. Oh, it felt so good. The forbidden aspect of it all.

I didn't care about Shondra while Savon was doing his thing to my body. All I cared about was the ecstasy I was feeling. It was driving me crazy. I spread my knees and put my face on the bed, twerking into his lap while he fucked me like a grown ass man, giving me back shots.

"Daddy-Daddy. I'm finna cum, I'm finna cum, Daddy! Aww, Savon, you my, Daddy. You my, Daddy, now!" I screamed and came all over his tool.

He wasn't far behind, twenty slams later, he gripped my ass, and pulled his dick out of me, cumming all over my ass cheeks. He opened my booty and nutted all over my anal ring before we collapsed onto the bed tonguing each other down. He gripped my ass and played all in my kitty driving me wild.

After we settled down, I hugged up to him and laid my head on his chest. He kissed my forehead and made me feel so good. "Tell me something, Baby Girl. Ain't this a better relationship than the one you got with, Carl?" He asked sucking on my neck.

Instead of answering his question, I pushed him on his back and straddled his body. "I don't know, but what I do know is that we about to have some fun." And we did that night, and every night so far. I couldn't get enough of Savon especially when he forced me.

Bi-curious

I don't care what nobody say if you ask me every female got a little bit of bi-curious in them, including me. I'd always been able to look at another female and give her props if she was beautiful. Or if I liked something she wore. That was natural for me. I could even acknowledge a nice figured woman and wouldn't feel no type of way about it. I didn't really think any of these things made me necessarily bi-curious, but then, if a dude was to do the same thing, I guess that would make people look at him like he was a little questionable in the heterosexual department. I guessed it should have been the same for a female. I don't know, what I do know is that I discovered I was bi-curious the day I met my fiancée's mother, Janet.

Janet was about five-feet-seven-inches tall, one-hundred and forty pounds, with light skin, and gray eyes like him. She had her hair cut into a short style that accentuated her pretty face. She reminded me of a prettier version of Nicole Murphy. They had damn near the same body type, but Janet's booty was slightly bigger. I'm only five-feet-three inches tall, one-hundred and thirty pounds. I have dark brown skin and brown eyes. Not a whole lot of booty, but I get some looks. Most of the glances from males go right to my double D breasts though.

After being engaged to my Fiancée, Norman for eight months, he took a job working as a D.J. for a local strip club. Things began to go down south for us to say the least. No more than two weeks after he'd started working at the club, we began arguing about almost everything. Where once I'd had unlimited access to his phone, now he'd changed the password and locked me out of it, and his Facebook account. He'd come home at all odd hours of the night. Then he'd get mad at me for waiting up for him.

It seemed like he had a habit of picking arguments, then disappearing for days on end. I didn't know what to do, or where to turn. I wanted to confide in my mother, but after she found out I was going to be taking a year off from college to get some things in order with my life, and that during that period I'd gotten engaged to Norman well, let's just say we weren't on speaking terms. Not knowing which way to turn, or where to go I decided to confide in Norman's mother, Janet. She and I would stay up into the wee hours of the night, on Facebook, or Snap Chat, talking and sharing pictures as if we were the best of friends and I honestly felt like we were. There was nothing I couldn't go to her about. Nothing I felt we kept from each other.

She gave me positive advice on how to handle a man like her son. She told me to always make sure I was keeping myself and my worth first. To never allow a man to take advantage of my heart and my mind, no matter how much I loved them. That went for her son as well. Some of the advice she gave me had me looking at my relationship with her son in a new light. I felt ever since he and I had been together that I had never placed myself first or considered my feelings when it came to him. I allowed Norman to do whatever he wanted to do, whenever he wanted to do it as long as he came home every night. I thought for a long time that was all that mattered. That was until she and I started to have our little talks.

Finally, after looking over things through the eyes of a mature, empowered woman. I waited one Sunday morning until Norman came into the house at 4 a.m. and gave him a piece of my mind. I told him how I was feeling, what I'd been thinking, and that I didn't appreciate how he'd been taking my kindness for weakness for as long as he'd been working at the club. In response, he brushed past me and left back out the house slamming the door behind him. I was devastated. I didn't know what he was thinking. What he was about to do. Or when and if he was coming black.

I was sick, I sat in the middle of the floor of our living room for a long time crying my eyes out. I loved him so much and couldn't stand being without him. Finally, I Facebooked Janet, and she invited me over to her place for a bit of a girl's night. She answered the door wearing a pair of cut off denim shorts that showed off a lot of her thighs, and a tank top without a bra, with a glass of wine in her hand that she handed to me.

"Aw, baby, how are you?" She asked hugging me.

I shook my head, as soon as I stepped into her arms the waterworks began. "I think he's cheating, Janet. He stays out until all hours of the night. Sometimes he doesn't come home at all. Then when he finally does, I ask him where he's been, and he never responds. He treats me like crap, and our sex life is nonexistent. I feel like he no longer wants me after seeing all those other girls at the strip club that he works at. Life just really sucks for me right now." I cried letting it all pour out.

Janet rubbed my back. "It's okay, baby. I'm here for you. Everything is going to be, okay." She pulled me further into the house. "I was just about to go outside for a swim. I want you to join me. Swimming is like one of the most therapeutic things you can do when you're feeling how, you're feeling, right now. Come on, let's get you into a better of state of mind. We'll spend the whole weekend restoring your strength. Then we'll deal with that son of mind. Damn, he's just like his rotten father it sounds like." She sighed out loud.

I shrugged my shoulders. "I didn't bring a bathing suit."

She waved me off. "It's okay, baby, it's just us girls here. You don't need one. Hey, if it makes you feel any better, I won't wear one either. How does that sound?" She brushed my hair out of my face and kissed my cheek, then grabbed my hand. Her expansive backyard was equipped with a meter pool. We stepped out into the beaming sun and walked alongside the pool hand in hand. "Come on, Sweetie, let's get you undressed." She stepped in front of me and pulled my tight blouse over my head and tossed it onto the Umbrella table. She looked down at the swell of my breasts and bucked her eyes. "Wow, those really are something, aren't they?"

I felt a bit shy, I don't know why, but I just did. Maybe it was because of how intense she was looking at them. "Yeah, I've had them ever since I was twelve years old."

She smiled. "If I were my son, I'd never be able to tear my lips away from them. They're wonderful." She ran her hands over the globes, squeezing them. "You're sure these are real?" she joked.

She kneeled down and pulled my skirt down my legs and laid it on the table on top of my blouse.

"Yeah, I'm sure!" I blushed.

I stepped in front of her and helped pull her tank top over her head. Her natural breasts bounced on her chest.

Cum For Me 4

They were nice and golden. The nipples were brown and covered with a nice amount of her globes. I couldn't take my eyes away from them.

She sucked her bottom lip. "Well, are you going to say something about these?" She shook her body from side to side. Her big breasts shook on her chest.

I swallowed, with my eyes bugged out of my head. "They are perfect. Honestly, I hope mine look that good a few years from now."

She slid her thumbs into the waistband of her cut off denims and slid them down her frame. She stood before me in her naked glory. She came over and pulled my panties down to my ankles, kneeling to complete the process. Her face wound up right in my crotch.

She sniffed it loudly. "Mmm, how can my son keep his hands off you? You smell as good as you look. Come on baby."

She took my hand and led me into the pool. We took one step at a time until the water came up to my neck. She wrapped her arms around my shoulders. Our boobies pressed against one another's. My hard nipples poked at hers, it felt odd, and at the same time incredibly arousing.

She looked into my eyes. "Baby, sometimes us girls have to take care of ourselves. We can't depend on a man to do everything for us. You understand me?" She took my hair and brushed it out of my face again.

I nodded my head, even though I wasn't sure what she meant entirely. "Yes, Janet, it's just so hard to not grow dependent on the man that you love. I mean have you ever been in love with a man who made you do and except some crazy things?"

She closed her eyes and rubbed her titties all over mine. Moaned deep within her throat. I could feel her hard nipples pricking me. They were fully engorged. They looked like they belonged on a baby's bottle. Her hands came up and squeezed mine together. "His father was the same way darling. He was a businessman. Made millions investing in banks, and real estate." She ran her face over my nipples and kissed them both one at a time. "Before he was rolling in the dough, we were forced to live in the Projects. I bussed my ass, worked two jobs and turned over all my money to help him make it through Business School. While we were living in the Projects, we had the strongest relationship you could ever imagine. After he became successful, though, that's when it all changed. Our relationship went downhill." She slid her hands down to my ass, squeezed my cheeks, and bumped her mound up against mine. "Mmm!"

I felt her hand go under and in between my thighs. Then her fingers traced the lining of my slit. She spread the lips with two of her fingers. My eyes closed, and my breathing intensified.

"His first purchase was this mansion, and a new Mercedes, one for him, and another for me. He gave me a credit card and had no problem with me spending thousands of dollars a week. For most girls that would have been the life, but not for me. I wanted more than the materialistic aspects of love. I wanted him, I wanted his devotion, his faithfulness, his commitment to our relationship and foundation. But all I got was an empty bed at night, and a closet full of clothes that could never suffice the pain he'd placed in my heart due to his neglection of the Eve in me." She slid two fingers into my sex and licked along the side of my neck.

She walked me backward until I was up against the side of the pool where the water was shallow.

I moaned into her mouth. "Janet, what are you doing?" More kissing. "Are you sure this is okay?"

Her fingers pushed further into me. She dragged her nose across my cheek and sucked my lips into her juicy ones. "Touch me Aleeyah, it's okay. Touch me and appreciate the woman that's me. Let me heal you as only a woman can." She stuck her tongue into my mouth and pulled me closer to her.

I very timidly slid my hands down her lower back and squeezed her rounded booty. It felt so soft in my hands. I tried to envision myself as a man while I rubbed all over it. What joy they must experience while hitting that big ole' thing from the back. I cuffed it like she was doing mine, and slid my hand between her cheeks, feeling her thick lips that were tucked under them. My fingers traced up and down her slit. I was afraid to press a finger into her. Scared that it would have been going too far. After all, she was my Fiancée's mother.

She moaned into my mouth and spread her legs. "Oh, baby, please put it in there. Let me feel it, it's okay." Her tongue licked all over my lips. She turned around and bent over in front of me. Her big booty glistened in the sunlight. She looked over her shoulder at me. "Finger me, baby. trust me, you'll love it."

I fearfully sucked two of my fingers into my mouth, then slowly slid them into her gap from the back. Her sex was overheated and tight around my digits. I pulled them out and then forced them back inside of her.

Getting a steady rhythm that I thought I'd like if I were being fingered in the fashion that she was.

She bounced back into them and moaned at the top of her lungs. "Oh-oh-oh-oh! That feels so good, so good, baby." She squeezed her breasts together and pulled the nipples from her mounds.

I continued to finger away at her until she tensed up and let out a guttural cry into the sky. Her walls sucked at my fingers, as cum squirted all around them. She turned around and kissed me on the lips, licking all over them.

She grabbed my breasts, pushing them together. "You have the prettiest titties I've ever seen on a young girl. You're so hot. My son is as stupid as his father." She licked around my areolas, then sucked them into her mouth one at a time. She placed her hand between my legs, and slipped two fingers up my pussy again, fingering me like an animal, digging deep into my body.

I was on my tippy toes, my ass crashed into the wall. My nipples had never been harder. "Janet-Janet-Janet, I can't take it! I'm gonna cum for you, I'm gonna cum," I whimpered.

Then it was happening, I came all over her fingers, while she jammed them into me and sucked my nipples.

* * *

Ten minutes later, she had me bent over the steps of the pool, while she rubbed a ten-inch strap-on up and down my vagina, holding my waist steady. "Okay, baby, now I'm going to show you why you don't ever need a man to do for you what another woman can do.

Give me this pussy." She humped forward and drove into me with so much force that I yelped.

"Oh, Janet, yes! Go-go-go, un! Yeah-yeah, go, deeper-deeper! I love it, damn, I love it!"

Janet placed one foot on the step that I was bent over, fucking me so hard tears welled in my eyes.

"Tell me-tell me- tell me, you don't need a man," She growled with her titties bouncing up and down.

I held on to the stair and pushed back into her. "I don't-I don't Janet, I swear, I don't. Oh, Lord, aw, you're killing me!"

I came so hard I almost fell face first into the water. She continued to work me. "Tell me-tell me, I can have this pussy, whenever I want it." She smacked my ass and continued to go hard on me.

I came and started shaking with drool sliding down my lip. "It's yours, it's yours. Anytime, anywhere, I swear! Oh!" I screamed.

My orgasm came from all over my body and had me convulsing. I'd never known a woman could make me cum so hard. She wiggled her thumb into my ass, and ran it in and out, then pulled the dildo out of me, and took it off.

"Come on, it's my turn now. I want you to take out all your frustrations on this pussy. You're the man, right now. Make me bow down to you."

* * *

We wound up getting out of the pool. She laid back on the lounge chair and opened her legs wide. "Come on baby, I need to feel those big titties against mine. Let me suck them while you fuck me into oblivion." She spread her lips showing me her pink.

I laid between her legs and probed for her opening with the big penis. It sank into her like a hot knife into butter. She moaned into my ear and wrapped her legs around me. Her nipples felt good against my own. Both of ours were poking at each other. It drove me crazy, I sucked her lips and tongue kissed her.

"This my pussy, Janet! You gone pay for what your son has done to me. You hear me!" I screamed.

I was fucking her so hard all she could do was whimper. The sounds of the dick going in and out of her kitty resonated in my ear. She was dripping wet, leaking over the both of us.

I felt like I was about to cum from hitting her cat so hard. I could feel the pressure on my clit and it was driving me literally insane. I started going crazy between her big thighs.

She sucked my nipples and squeezed the boobs together. "Un, that's how you do it, baby! That's how you take out your frustrations! Grab my neck!"

I didn't hesitate, I squeezed it, and continued to pound her out. "It's mine, Janet-mine!" I squeezed her throat so hard I was sure she couldn't breathe.

She opened her thighs wider and screamed breathlessly. "I'm cumming! I'm cumming, you little bitch! Aw fuck!" She yelled as her body shook violently.

She moaned with her lips wrapped around my hard, left nipple. Because I felt her cumming, it did something to me. I could no longer hold back. I came all over the dildo, grinding into her pussy.

She laid me on my back and ate me out while rubbing all over my titties. "I can't believe you made me cum like that. I can't believe it." She kissed my kitty and started sucking on the sex lips.

I closed my eyes, as she ate me through another orgasm. I came hollering for her to fuck me again. She got up and got into position, pushing my knees to my chest, when the patio door slid open.

Norman ran over to us with his hands against his cheeks. "Mom, what are you doing to my Fiancée?"

Ca$h & Company

Blackmailed and Spanked

I sat on the couch nervous as a hooker in church. I could not believe the Golden State Warriors had been up in the series against the Cleveland Cavaliers three games to one, and now they were seconds away from losing the entire series. I was horrified as I saw LeBron take the free throw line and make the last shot, pretty much sending the game out of reach for my Warriors.

As the final buzzer sounded, I lowered my head and looked across the living room at, Michael my husband's best friend. We made eye contact and he gave me a knowing smile. I cringed and felt sick to my stomach. My husband, Wayne, sat beside him drinking a beer unaware of what Michael and I had going on.

Three weeks prior to this day an old friend of mine by the name of, Troy had come into to town for a Medical conference here in Atlanta. Troy was a major power player in the Pharmaceuticals game. We'd dated for nearly two years before, Wayne and I had gotten engaged, and eventually married. Troy had been the love of my life until we went off to two different colleges. Once that happened, we started to drift apart and settled into the realm of friends with occasional benefits. I say occasional because after we went off to separate colleges, we were reduced to hooking up sexually once or twice a year. Although whenever we did, wow, it was always amazing.

Well, about three weeks ago, when Troy came into town, he and I had gotten together while my husband was out of town visiting relatives in California. I thought Troy and I would be able to spend the entire weekend together at the Four Seasons, have a good time, then he could be on his way back to New York, and I could go home and continue living my happily married life.

Well, unfortunately, that's not how things worked out. Michael, my husband's best friend since childhood just so happened to be entertaining one of the many dancers that work at his multiple clubs around the city at the Four Seasons that weekend. He spotted me there, hugged up with Troy at the bar downstairs. We made eye contact and once again he gave me that knowing smile and didn't say anything about it until two weeks later when Wayne got back into town. I could still remember the conversation as if it were yesterday.

Wayne had run off to the meat market to pick up a case of baby back smoked ribs, leaving me and Michael alone in the house. Michael didn't wait until Wayne pulled all the way out of the driveway before he approached me in the kitchen as I was washing the dishes with my big yellow latex gloves on. He came behind me and wrapped his arms around my waist, causing me to jump.

"Hey, Trina, you know we got some things to talk about, right?" He ground the front of his crotch into my backside. I could feel his manhood through the denim of his pants and my short skirt.

I took his arms from around me and pushed him away from me. "Get away from me, dude. What's the matter with you?" I asked with a frown on my face that should have told him I meant business.

He laughed. "Aw hell naw. You ain't about to come at me like that today. You see I got the upper hand, now.

I'm gone get what I been wanting from your lil' fine yellow ass." He licked his lips.

The whole time Wayne and I had been together, Michael had always been a problem trying to get at me from the sidelines. He and I had gone out on a few dates back in college, but nothing had come from them. Though I found him handsome, very charming, and well put together, Michael was a hoe. He had way too many women circling around him. I just knew that he would never take me seriously or make me a priority in his life. Whereas Wayne was great at doing just that. I was one of those type of females who needed to be put first. I couldn't have it any other way.

"You know I saw you the other day with that, Troy nigga, right?" *My heart skipped a beat. I felt like I was about to hyperventilate.*

"Yeah, I saw you at the Four Seasons, but it wasn't what you thought it was. Troy and I were just hanging out, that's all. I love Wayne with all my heart, you know I do." *I brushed past him and continued to wash the dishes in the sink.*

Michael stepped behind me again and put his lips in my ear. "If there was nothing to it. Why haven't you told my mans about you and, Troy yet, then? I'm pretty sure you wouldn't have a problem with me telling him then, huh?"

I turned around to face him. I was worried, I couldn't lose my husband. I loved Wayne with all my heart, but Troy had this unexplainable hold on me. One that he'd had ever since he'd taken my virginity in the ninth grade. As much as I loved my husband there was something that made me flock to Troy whenever I knew he was within reach. I can't explain why that was, it was just a fact. I wasn't perfect, I took a deep breath, looking up into his brown eyes, and dark-skinned face.

His goatee was freshly shaped along with the low-cut mohawk hairstyle he was rocking. He smelled like Cool Water cologne. I hadn't smelled that scent on a man in a number of years. I'd always liked it. I tried to exhale as hard as I could to get the scent of him out of my nose.

"What do you want me from me, Michael? Just come on out with it?"

He flipped me around and bent me over the sink with blazing speed. Then he raised my skirt and rubbed all over my booty, squeezing the cheeks. "I been watching this ass get bigger and bigger ever since college. It ain't a finer one in all of Atlanta and trust me I been looking. I wanna spank this. You let me spank this ass and I swear, I won't say nothing to, Wayne, about what I know you and Troy did all that weekend. It'll just be our lil' secret. What you think about that?" He slid his fingers into the crack of my ass, pinched my thong and moved it to the side.

I reached behind me and smacked his hand away. "Have you lost your mind? A spanking, what do I look like to you?" I snapped.

"A finer, more strapped version of Ashanti? Any more questions?" He laughed looking down at me.

I wiggled my skirt as far down as it could go. "I can't let you do that to me, Michael. That's weird, besides, I can't sin against, Wayne like that, and you're his best friend. Where is your loyalty?" I bumped him out of my way and threw my gloves on the kitchen table.

He snatched me up and slammed me into the refrigerator. "I'm not the one that married him, you did. Now,

I can't help how I feel about this body. Look at it, if you worked in one of my clubs, you'd take home no less than ten gees every night. I know that for a fact. Everybody loves red bones, especially when they're strapped like you are. Man, just look at you."

Once again, I broke out of his embrace. "Well, you're not supposed to be looking at me, Michael. I'm not your woman. I belong to, Wayne. I'm not about to let you spank me. That ain't, right."

He stepped in front of me and grabbed my arms. "Alright, how about this. You like them, Warriors, right? Steph and all them?"

I nodded. "Yeah, what about them?"

"Well, you know my dude is, Lebron. "How about we make a little wager. I say Lebron, and the Cleveland Cavaliers beat your squad this year and Lebron brings Cleveland home a ring. If he do, you gotta let me spank you, but if they lose, we'll forget all about what happened at the Four Seasons. I'll never come at you bogus again. It's gon' be hard, but I'ma do it. What do you say?" He asked letting my arms go.

"You know they're already down one game, right? Ain't gon' be no bullshit, because of that?" I asked liking the sound of this.

He smiled. "Yeah, I know, so the odds are in your favor. Do we have a deal?"

I exhaled and nodded my head reluctantly. "Yeah, we got a deal."

Now flashing back to the current day. I sat on the couch devastated. I couldn't understand how they had managed to lose a series where they were up three games to none. It was unheard of. Michael waited until Wayne left the house to drop off two of his other friends before sliding next to me on the couch. I was still sitting there with my head down, lost. I didn't know what to do. I felt like running and never looking back.

He snickered. "Welp, a deal is a deal. I guess I'll be seeing you at my Mansion out in Monona. And don't worry, I ain't gon' beat on that big 'ole thang back there too hard. But I know for a fact, before it's all said and done, you're gonna beg me to fuck you. Watch!"

I jerked my head back. "What, no, Michael. I agreed to a light spanking. We're not having sex. I'm letting you know that, right now," I said jumping up and mugging him with mounting anger.

He laughed. "What's crazy is that I don't even wanna fuck. I just wanna get acquainted with that treasure under your lower back." He rose from the couch and grabbed his jacket. "I'll text you the information and let the gatekeeper know when you'll be coming. I can't wait."

I flopped back on the couch with my face in my hands. "What the fuck have I gotten into?" I cursed myself.

* * *

I waited a week before I decide to honor my end of the bet. It was a Saturday night and I'd convinced Wayne that I'd be having a girl's night out with my best friend Kelah. I'd already told her I needed her to cover for me in case Wayne called. She said she'd have my back with no questions asked. Then paused and told me she wanted all the dirty details later before hanging up the phone.

When I arrived at Michael's mansion, he greeted me at the door with a bottle of wine and a blunt. "I know you used to smoke a little bit in college. I don't know if you still do, but I think now is as good of a time as any. That way you can relax and just let things happen naturally."

I bumped him out of the way and stepped into his palace. "There is nothing natural about this, Michael. You are asking to spank my ass like I'm some unruly child. It's nuts, let's just get this shit over with, please." I'd been to his place more than a few times with Wayne, so I pretty much knew my way around it. I headed up the white carpeted spiral staircase and down the long hall that had a bunch of expensive paintings along it. "Where are we doing this at, Michael? In your bedroom I assume?" I hollered over my shoulder to him.

He shook his head. "Naw, Ma, we'll be in the guestroom. If you go into that bedroom we're screwing. I'm telling you that, right now." He opened the door to the guestroom and waited for me to walk through it.

I stopped in front of him and looked into his eyes. "Listen to me, nigga. I don't know what you think this is, but I ain't going for it. You will never get none of this body. I may have stepped out on Wayne with, Troy, but I have my own reasons for that. I will not cross him with you." I rolled my eyes as I entered the room.

It was huge, dark, and filled with lit candles. It smelled like Somali Rose. The sounds of *Jhene Aiko's Psilocybin* played through the speakers. She was my favorite singer, I don't know how Michael knew that. He had red rose petals spread across the bed and a big Gucci pillow in the middle of it.

He walked behind me and placed his chin on my shoulder. "Shall we begin?" He handed the glass around to me.

I took it and drained it. "I guess now is as good of a time as any. What do you want me to do?"

"Nothing, from here on out. I'll take care of everything!" He dropped down behind me and rose my tight skirt above my waist. Then rubbed both hands from the bottom of my right ankle, all the way to the top of my thigh, stopping along the back of my satin panties.

"On second thought, I think I will take a few tokes of that blunt. I need to center myself." That's just what I did. After the tenth pull, I was floating on air. My eyes were low, and all my senses were heightened.

Michael sat on the bed and pulled me over his lap with my skirt above my waist. He took his big hand and rubbed it all over my booty cheeks. "I swear you got a perfect ass, Trina. I ain't never seen nobody with one so round and fat like this." He leaned his face down and kissed it.

"Michael, none of that, just do what you gotta do. So, I can get off you and back home. Come on, now." I situated myself and laid back down. My heart thumped in my chest, I was fearful of the unknown.

"A'ight then, here we go." He raised his hand and brought it down right in the center of my cheeks, hard. I could feel them jiggle, along with my thighs. The pain shot all the way up my spine, and before I could get used to it, he smacked them again in the same spot. "Yeah, how you luv that?"

I bit into my bottom lip and squeezed my eyelids together. "Not so hard, Michael. That hurts," I whimpered.

He smacked me again, this time just on the right side of my booty. Then the left, then the right again. He went back and forth until I felt like my seat was on fire. I tried to get up, but he had me trapped around the waist, and my legs.

I could feel his penis hardening under my stomach. He paused for a second and gripped my backside, kneading them like dough. He pulled them apart and circled a wet finger around my anus, after pulling my panties all the way to one side. "Damn, Trina, you so thick. I swear you thick." He brushed his finger over my kitty lips. Then pulled my panties back in place. "It looks like you getting wet to me, Trina. You sure this ain't turnin' you on even a lil' bit?" He asked this question with a handful of my cheeks in his right hand.

"Hell naw," I quivered. "This is sick. Just finish and get it over with." My thighs were shaking. I could feel my sex swelling. I didn't think it was possible for such an act to turn me on. I was starting to think that I had some serious issues.

"Alright then." He smacked me three hard times in a row. Then stopped and rubbed my booty. He slapped the cheeks five times in a row, repeating the same process. After a series of seven slaps. He pulled my panties all the way down to the bottom of my ankles and off. "Now, I'm really finna show you how I get down." He spread my legs, ran his hand into my center, and opened my lips briefly, collecting my juices, rubbing them on my ass.

Smack! Smack! Smack!

He went on a rampage, over and over again, warming my bottom with his heavy hands. Every time his hand crashed into me, my ass would jiggle, and send what felt like an electric current right to my clitoris.

I got one leg free and kicked it wildly. "Michael, stop, stop! Oh, please stop! Aww, my God, it hurts! Oh—Michael," I groaned feeling my juices leaking out of me in rivers.

Michael was relentless, his hand showed me no mercy. He'd slap first my left cheek, and then the right. Before slapping it right in the middle above my kitten. The vibration traveled directly to my vagina's nipple and sent shivers all through me. It got so bad, I unconsciously humped into his hard penis that was poking me through his pants.

He paused, opened my lips and circled my clit with his middle finger, before resuming slap after slap across my ass. I could feel his dick grow underneath me from each blow. I tried to reposition myself so that my clit could rub against it, but his grip on me was just too tight. I was about to lose my mind.

"Michael! Michael! Oh, please touch me. Michael, please, I'm begging you!" I cried humping against his pants leg as he continued to spank me with no remorse.

He stopped and rubbed my booty again, then squeezed both cheeks in his hands, and thumbed my clitoris that had found its way outside of my kitty lips. I screamed and started to shake. I was praying he would slide a finger in me. I needed it so bad, my thighs were drenched, and so was his lap.

Whap! He ignored my requests and went back to spanking me instead. When he was done, he pushed me off his lap, knocking me to the floor. "A'ight, now, get yo' shit and get out!" he snapped. "Your debt is paid."

I got up and stood on wobbly legs and grabbed his wrists. My juices poured out of me like never before. "Please, fuck me, Michael. Please, you can't leave me like this! I'ma go crazy!" I slid my hand between my legs rubbing my swollen cat.

I needed him so bad and I could see his hard dick sticking through his pants. It looked like it was huge. Word on campus was that he was hung like an elephant's trunk. I didn't know if I could take it all, but I wanted to try. "Please, fuck me!"

He unzipped his pants and pulled his dick out. The girls had not lied, it was huge. He stroked it. "Let's go."

The next thing I knew, I was bent over his bed in the master bedroom. He had my cheeks opened wide licking in between them I had my face laid sideways on his covers trying to look back at him. Everything he was doing was feeling so good that I felt like screaming. He held my hips and stuck his entire face into my gap. Then sucked my pussy lips into his mouth and slurped at them like they were raw Oysters.

"Cum for me, Trina. Cum for me so I can kill this pussy like a Savage." He pinched my clit and pulled it.

That was all it took. I started to cum so hard I fell to the bed humping his cover like a maniac. I pulled my nipples, then rose back to all fours. Just as Michael got behind me and yanked my head backward by my hair. I felt his hard dick forcing its way into my body. He began fucking me so hard all I could do was grab a handful of the covers.

"Uh-Michael-Michael! Please, baby, aw shit-aw shit!" I was breathing hard, trying not to pass out.

His dick was so far in me I felt like I could taste it. The bed rocked back and forth, and all I could do was see my husband's face in my mind as his best friend slung his pipe to me. I felt so guilty. Michael smacked me on the ass and forced me on to my side. Then he took a hold of my right leg and held it in his forearm. My juices coated his bat as it stroked in and out of me. My lips were so swollen that they were red. The sight brought on a strong orgasm. I couldn't help screaming, as he fucked me harder and harder.

"I told you! I told you-I told you. You was gon' beg for this!" He bragged fucking me harder and harder. "Didn't I-didn't I? Shit, I'm cumming! I'm cumming, Trina!"

He flipped me on my back and pushed my knees to my chest, fucking me hard and fast. From this position, I couldn't move. I was trapped. I'd never been more filled, another orgasm ripped through me, then I felt his cum in large jets splashing into my womb. I came again. We stayed entangled for what felt like an eternity. Finally, Michael slid out of me, turned me on my stomach, and rammed my ass out for the next thirty minutes like he couldn't get enough. I didn't know where things were headed between us after this night, but I knew for sure I'd be looking to place some more bets against him hoping to lose.

While He's Out Cheating

"See, girl, I told you. I wouldn't lie to you, that nigga is trifling." Dominique said rubbing my back.

I fixed the lenses on the binoculars, so I could zoom into my husband Marcus's side piece's window. I couldn't believe they hadn't had enough decency to pull the blinds. They had to be the stupidest, most careless people in all of Virginia Beach.

"Yeah, girl had I not seen this I would have never believed it. This the same bitch he told me was his cousin. Damn, niggas are so trifling." I sighed and sat back in the seat of my two weeks old 2019 Mercedes Benz truck that Marcus had just bought me for our two-year wedding anniversary.

"Kylie, I told you, you be giving him way too much of your power. That nigga ain't even all that." Dominique looked out of the window at the house with a mug on her face. She snapped her fingers for the binoculars and I handed them to her.

"It ain't just that, Dominique, that's my husband. We took vows together before, God. That means everything to me. I ain't going to hell because of him." I was serious about that.

I knew God would not play about a woman disobeying, or not honoring her husband. I did not want the good Lord's wrath to come down on my head, I was afraid of that.

"Aw, hell naw, where she come from? This nigga got two bitches up there with him, and they both all over this fool. Look!"

I was feeling sick before I even grabbed the binoculars back. I honestly didn't want to see it, but part of me knew I had to see it in order to believe it. Once I placed the tool back on my eyes and confirmed what Dominique had said to be true, I lost my mind. Before I could stop myself, I was out of that truck and running across the street with Dominique calling my name at the top of her lungs. I wasn't trying to hear none of that. My mind was made up.

I rushed up the porch steps and tried the knob on the door. To my surprise it was open. My heart skipped a beat as I rushed inside and headed straight up the stairs. I kicked their mutt of a dog out of my way then took the stairs two at a time. When I got to the top of them, I could hear one of the bitches moaning like he was killing her. That pissed me off, I knew my man was an animal in the sack. He'd been blessed with more dick than common sense. All the years that we'd been together, I'd never suspected him of cheating. I'd been with him when we were struggling and living on just my one paycheck while he attended college and played basketball.

I put my dreams on hold so that he could move forward with his. Now, that he'd been drafted in the overall four pick by the Philadelphia Seventy-Sixers, I guess he felt he could do me like this. Well, he had another thing coming. I ran into the door that I suspected him of being in with the homewreckers and bussed through it with my shoulder, falling to my knees.

"Marcus Garvey Washington! What the fuck are you in here doing!" I screamed from the carpet.

The two white girls yelled and rushed to hide behind him. He scrambled to find his boxers, while the white girl's fake boobs bounced around on their smoked Lobster colored chests. The room smelled like wet dog, pussy, sweat, and weed smoke. I wanted to throw up. I climbed to my feet and made my way toward him swinging wildly. Not only was he cheating on me, but he was doing it with two white girls after swearing to me he didn't even like white women. Man was I hurt, I felt like I didn't know this man.

Our whole relationship had revolved around the beautiful dark skin that he swore up and down he loved. Now I was starting to question if he'd really liked it at all. I felt so worthless, and ugly. My whole life so many people had made fun of my dark complexion, it got so bad I began to feel like I was flawed. Then came Marcus. In high school, he'd write me poems about how beautiful I was every single day.

"Baby, I can explain, I was just—" Marcus started, but it was too late.

My fists were hitting him everywhere they could connect. His face, head, shoulders, arms. I went psycho.

Dominique came and grabbed me off him. "Kylie, chill, that ain't gon' solve nothing. He still gon' be a cheating dog when it's all said and done," she snapped.

The white girls slid under the bed. I could hear them whimpering. I had a mind to pull their asses from under there. But I knew how Virginia was. They were racist in this state. Far as I knew they'd have me up under the jail. I couldn't afford a felony on my record. I was in my second year of medical school. A felony would have shattered my dreams of becoming a surgeon.

Marcus backed away from the bed holding his face. "Yo', I knew you had to be involved. Kylie this broad hate men. She's a fuckin lesbian. She trying to turn you against me. That's all this is!" He hollered pointing at Dominique. His big dick swung from right to left in front of his muscular thighs. He stopped and put his boxers back on.

"Naw, nigga, don't put that shit on me. You up here fucking these two white bitches. I just had to let her know what was good. She's my best friend."

He waved her off and made his way over to me. "Baby, this bitch just wanna fuck wit' you on the low. I'm telling, you, that's the only reason she always in our business. You gotta believe me. It's not what you think." He grabbed my right hind.

I slapped the shit out of him with my left, knocking him down on one knee. "You think I'm stupid, Negro? You're up here cheating on me and trying to blame it on somebody else You know what, Marcus, I love you! And you're my everything, but I need some space. I gotta think things over. I'm so fucking hurt, right now, it ain't funny." Tears fell from my eyes, I wiped them away. I didn't want him to see me cry. I couldn't give him that satisfaction.

"Baby, what can I do? I'll do anything. Do you want another truck? A shopping spree with the Black card, a week's vacation? What, Boo, just name it?" he pleaded.

I scoffed and made my way out of the room, stopping in the doorway. "Marcus, I'ma get all those things anyway. So, you can come up with something better than that. Don't come home tonight, I need to think."

* * *

When I got home, I opened a bottle of red wine, sat on my couch, and broke down like never before. I couldn't think of any reason for Marcus to have been out cheating on me. I'd always tried to be the best woman I possibly could to him. I'd been faithful, supportive, and his number one fan way before he was drafted to any NBA. I just didn't get why he chose to hurt the Queens that stood by his side since day one.

All for what, a few hours of passion with women that didn't give two fucks about him. It was idiotic, it made no sense. I felt so ugly and discarded. I started to wonder why my skin had to be so dark. Why couldn't I have been a yellow female? I couldn't recall anyone of them that had been cheated on. The majority of Marcus's new NBA friends were either married to light skinned exotic looking females, Spanish girls, or white women. I don't think any of them had a dark-skinned sista like myself. Maybe I was out of my league. Maybe he wasn't in the wrong, I was. For being as dark as I was, I hated me at that moment. I couldn't help feeling extremely low.

Dominique came over and slid next to me on the couch. She wrapped her arm around my shoulder and pulled me close to her. "I hate when you get like this. That nigga ain't all that, Kylie. You are a Queen. I keep telling you that. You are so beautiful you could have anybody you want in this world." She kissed my cheek, then rubbed it away with her thumb.

"Don't nobody want me. I'm too fucking dark. Don't none of the women in our new circle look like me. I'm not in their league. It's not his fault, it's only a matter of time before he leaves me altogether. I just know it."

"Then it would be his loss, and I gotta tell you. You are the most beautiful woman in the world. Ain't nobody on our level. You're smart, funny, you have an amazing personality, and on top of that you're sexy, with a body that makes females get a hard-on," she joked.

I snickered, smiled and took a deep breath. "Thank you for saying that. I just wish it were the truth." I blew air out of my jaws and lowered my head.

Dominique slid off the couch and kneeled in front of me. "You wanna know the only truthful thing that came out of his mouth all night?" She asked, placing her hand on my face, wiping away my tears with her thumb.

I sniffed snot back into my nose. "What's that because I thought everything, he said was a damn lie?"

"Well, I do have a thing for you. I do want to be with you, if only for a night. I'm not trying to change the atmosphere of our relationship or make things complicated, but I want you. I have ever since we were little girls and were each other's first kisses." She smiled and looked into my eyes.

I was shocked that she said that so boldly. She and I had been best friends for as long as I could remember. Our mothers had bathed us in the same sink when we were kids. We had numerous sleepovers together. Took showers together, but never once had I ever felt she had a thing for me. Dominique had been a lesbian ever since she was real little. Even back then all her girlfriends were the finest in the school, or on the block. They were so pretty I used to feel insecure just being in the same room with them. I knew for a fact, I was nowhere on their level. So, I never thought I had even crossed her mind.

"Dominique, so are you saying he was right? That the only reason you took me there was to break us apart?" I didn't know how I felt about that. Apart of me felt betrayed and even hurt.

"Absolutely not. I took you there because I was tired of him getting over on you. While you thinking that he was doing right by you, when he wasn't. You're my best friend. It's my job to watch out for your well-being. Is it not?" I had a million thoughts going through my mind and didn't know what to say to her.

Before I could get my thoughts together to respond, Marcus came into the house and froze by the door. "Baby can I talk to you. I don't—"

"Marcus stay over there, or I swear to God, I'll divorce your ass and take half of everything!" I hollered.

He was about to take a step but didn't He placed his back against the door, looking across the room at us. "Baby, can we just talk for a minute? I know I fucked up, I'll give anything to make it up to you. You can have whatever you like. I—"

"Marcus, shut up," I snapped. "Just stand there and don't move." I looked down at Dominique. "Dominique, will you take me just for one night. Heal me, sis, huh?"

She nodded. "You already know I got you." She ran her hands over my exposed thighs. Then forced my Gucci dress up my legs even further. She kissed my knee, and sucked on the right one, kissing along my inner thigh. "This skin is so beautiful." Her tongue ran back and forth, then her lips came together sucking.

"Baby, I know you ain't finna make me stand here and watch you do this? Please, let's just talk about it." He started to make his way in our direction.

"Marcus, I swear to God if you move from that spot one more time, you're going to regret it. Now stay there!"

Dominique, pushed my Gucci dress all the way up, sucking my inner thighs. I could feel her teeth dragging across them, it had my panties soaking wet. I'd never thought about my friend in this light, but now that she was doing her thing. I could not help but be aroused in a major way. I think, the aspect of Marcus watching also added to the spiciness of it all. He was reaping what he had sown, as very well he should have.

"Kylie stand up real fast," She breathed with her hot breath.

I stood before her. She reached under my dress and pulled my thongs down and off my bare feet. She sat me back down on the couch and draped my right leg over the arm of it.

She sniffed my box, planting her nose right on my crease. "Damn, girl, you smell so good. I could sniff you forever and never get tired."

She peeled my lips apart and licked up and down in between them. Then rubbed her face over my cat. "Shit, Kylie, it's good baby. It tastes so good."

I arched my back and moaned. "Dominique, go ahead, heal me. Make me cum. Make me cum while his trifling ass watches! I need you so bad."

She nipped at my clit with her teeth. Took two fingers and slid them into my sex. Driving them in and out of me. "Kylie, cum on my tongue. I wanna swallow you, baby. You're so damn fine," She said between pauses of licking me.

I forced her head into my gap, and wrapped my thighs around her head, trapping her. I felt her sucking my clit like a nipple and couldn't stop from cumming hard.

"Dominique-Dominique! Aw shit, baby I'm cumming. I'm cumming!" I humped into her mouth shaking like crazy.

She licked all over my bald chocolate kitty, sucking on the lips and pulling them somewhat from my mound. She stood up and dropped her pants.

"I'm about to show this nigga, how to fuck, I got you, Kylie!" She pulled open my legs and dropped her boxers.

The ten-inch dildo she kept strapped on at all times flopped out in front of her. It looked like it was as thick as my wrist. She got between my thighs and worked the head into my tight hole. She started wiggling from side to side.

"Damn, this pussy tight. I don't know if I'ma be able to get all the way in here." I bit into my bottom lip as I felt more and more of her going inside of me.

I looked over her shoulder to see Marcus with his dick out, stroking it as if he'd lost his mind. I sucked her neck and closed my eyes. "Force it, Dominique, and fuck me. I need you." I spread my thighs as far as I could, feeling her sink deeply into me, hitting my bottom. "Uh, Baby!"

I moaned digging my nails into her back. She pulled out of me and slammed it back home. Then her rhythm was all savage. She hooked my thigh over her arm.

"This how you hit this pussy, Marcus! You see this shit—" She huffed and puffed screwing the living daylights out of me.

The couch scooted backward and bumped into the wall. The lamp fell off the table that was next to us.

Dominique looked over her shoulder at, Marcus, as she continued to fuck me.

"Dominique, baby! Aw, shit. Yes-yes hit this pussy. I don't need, him! I don't need, him," I moaned.

I rose up and kissed her lips, had I known she could put it down like she was. I would have probably tried her out for size a long time ago. I mean even though, it had never crossed my mind, it was now. I laid all the way on top of me and sawed her piece in and out of me. Hitting one wall, then the other.

"Tell me you gon' cum, Kylie. Tell me, I can feel your pussy sucking at me." She got to going super hard and put both of my legs over her shoulders working me over.

I couldn't take it, I had to cum. I had to, it felt so good. I closed my eyes and let out a guttural scream. Then came all over her and opened my eyes just in time to see Marcus cumming in his fist. He fell to his knees still stroking himself. Cum shot across the carpet. She pulled out of me, kneeled and ate me like a veteran bringing me to two more orgasms, before standing up and sticking her pole into my mouth allowing me to suck my juices off it. I had to admit that I tasted good.

Marcus crawled over to where we were. He laid his head on my thigh. "I'm sorry, baby. I swear, I ain't gon' cheat no more. I will never take you for granted anymore. Please forgive me, I am begging you."

Well, I didn't believe him then and I still don't now. While my husband is on the road, I don't know what he's out there doing, even though, he swears up and down he's being faithful. Whether he is or isn't, I can't get enough of Dominique and can't see myself giving her up anytime soon. I guess you can say what's good for the goose is good for the gander. I'm good. I'm focused on my studies and becoming the best possible me, in this beautiful, dark skin.

Ca$h & Company

The Gift of a Promotion

I couldn't take my eyes off one of the most beautiful Black women I'd seen in all my life, as she sat across the firm's conference table from me jotting down notes, while Ryan Eisenhower gave out the budget breakdowns for the last quarter.

I was supposed to be taking notes as well, but as long as Michelle was in the room, I could never maintain my focus. Michelle was a little under five-feet-six inches fall. She looked like she weighed no more than a hundred and thirty pounds. She had nice shoulder length hair, that was full of sheen. Her eyes were brown and so was her perfect skin. She had the kind of body that put most women to shame. A flat stomach, big butt, and nice boobs. She wore glasses, but even they couldn't take away from her obvious sex appeal.

I was in awe of this Goddess. I knew I would give her the world if she allowed me, too. Unfortunately, even though, I was a partner at my father's law firm, and on the verge of inheriting it outright, but Michelle acted as if I didn't exist. I watched her as she finished scribbling down her notes and bit the end of her pen, waiting for Ryan to continue with the breakdowns. She looked across the table at me, and smiled, before going back to her notes. That was all it took, and I was off to the bathroom with the need to relieve myself thinking about her gorgeous ass.

This went on for weeks. Every time I saw Michelle in passing, I would smile, or wave at her in the hopes that she would return my gestures, and each time she did, I felt the need to escape to the confines of the bathroom. Now I know most of you would find that very weird, or even somewhat sick, but I'm telling you if you saw how beautiful this woman was, you'd understand.

I was raised around nothing but rich, privileged white people. I didn't even see my first Black person physically until my first trial. I know that may seem impossible, but it's honest to God truth. So, not only was I mesmerized by Michelle's skin color, but she was this new kind of beauty. One that I was unaccustomed too. My infatuation with her grew into obsession fast. So, fast that even I hated it. It got to the point that the relationship with my wife had gone down the drain. Our sex life became nonexistent.

The only way I could stand to make love to her was if the lights were out, and R&B music was playing. On those nights I'd close my eyes tight, and imagine, Michelle. Boy did my wife reap the benefits of her image. I'd never heard her scream as loud. Then it happened—

Four months after I became a senior partner at my father's firm, he passed away and left the fifty-million-dollar business to the firm. I also inherited two beach houses, and his favorite Rolls Royce. It was one of the first times in my life where I was so glad to have been an only child. It took three additional months for his will to go into effect, but as soon as soon as it did, I went into effect.

***

A month after I took over the full reigns of the firm. I called Michelle in my office to have a sit-down. I didn't know what to say to her. I honestly just wanted to see her.

She sauntered into my office holding a laptop on her left hand. "Mr. Hupy, you wanted to see me?" She was dressed in a nice dark blue, Fendi business skirt suit. Her glasses matched the red bottom pumps she wore to offset her suit.

There was something about the way this woman dressed that appealed to the male fashionista in me. I'd tried for years to get my wife to dress in the manner that Michelle did, but she sucked at it. So, I stopped trying.

I signaled for her to come into my office. "Yes, and close that door behind you. Have a seat." She followed my commands.

She turned around showing off the swell of her ample backside. It stood out from her back like a sideways mountain. I felt myself getting hard.

She took a seat in front of me and crossed her thighs. Her Fendi skirt rose just enough to show me the hem of her white stockings. The sight drove me crazy. There was nobody like this black woman.

"Sir, can you tell me what this is pertaining too?" She asked pushing her glasses up on her nose.

I tried to get a hold of myself, but my cock was so hard it was hurting me. Her thighs were so juicy and perfect. Her face, like a brown-skinned porcelain doll. Her perfume flooded my office and placed me in a zone all on its own.

"Well, Michelle, before my father passed away, he had some really nice things to say about you. I understand that you and he had a very special relationship. One I'm sure you're going to miss. However, I can assure you that you and I can have an even better one. I've been meaning to invite you here so that we could have a formal sit down. I apologize for taking so long to do so." I didn't know what the hell I was saying.

My father had not told me about any relationship between him and Michelle. In fact, I don't even know if he knew that she worked here. Our firm held a staff of one hundred people. My father was very antisocial.

Michelle uncrossed her thighs and looked over her shoulder at the goings on outside of my office. You see, my office had two really big windows and the blinds that were pulled up.

She turned back to me and bit on her manicured nails. "Mr. Hupy, I don't know, what your father told you, but that was a one-time thing. He said he'd keep it to himself, and it's not the reason I made Junior Partner. I bust my ass here."

Oh my God, my heart was pounding. I felt like I'd struck gold.

I didn't know how I was going to play with this, but I knew I was. She looked nervous and worried. She crossed her thighs again, the hemline rose higher, exposing the bottom of her right cheek above the stocking.

I came from around my desk and lowered the blinds in my office. I was so hard, I knew I couldn't avoid her seeing me poked out the way that I was. I was so excited, I could barely breathe.

"Mr. Hupy, I assure you that I am a professional. If you've called me here to fire me, because of what your father may have told you. I am asking that you don't. I felt like I didn't have any other choice. I cared about him."

I stepped to the back of her chair and ran my hand across her shoulders. "Oh, I didn't call you in here to fire you, Michelle. I want to give you a promotion." I leaned down and sniffed her.

She smelled sweet, like forbidden fruit. Fruit that I'd been denied my entire life because of my stupid up-bringing. My father made it a habit of preaching about fidelity and keeping the family structure pure and strong. Here I was getting the gist that not only had he stepped out on my mother. He'd done so with a black woman and probably had been doing things like that for years. He was such a hypocrite.

"A promotion, but, Sir, I've only recently made Junior Partner. I haven't had the job for a month yet. I'm still getting acquainted with my work detail. I don't think I'm ready to be a Senior Partner." Michelle started biting on her fingernails again.

I laughed. "Who cares. The job pays two hundred and fifty thousand dollars a year. You'll have full bene-fits. A month of vacation time. And it comes with a two-thousand and nineteen Lexus truck." I placed my chin in the crease of her neck as I leaned over the back of her chair. "How does that sound?"

She looked at me from the corners of her eyes. "And what do you want in return. My mother always told me that if a white man is offering you something, he has a hidden agenda. It's best to find out what it is before you accept what he's offering. So, what's your deal, white boy?"

I stood up shocked, this was definitely a side of her I'd never seen before. I backed away. "Wait, why are you talking to me like that. I thought that you were afraid of me?"

She stood up and shook her head. "Naw, I can only play that role for so long. I'm not afraid of you. I wasn't afraid of your father either." She stepped into my face and backed me up against the wall in my office. She placed her hand on my chest. "So, why are you promoting me so fast? Hupy, what do you have in mind, or should I dare to guess?" She trailed her hand from my chest to my stomach, then all the way down to my crotch, cuffing me there.

I winced, and my dick got harder than it had ever been before. I couldn't believe this beautiful black Queen was touching me. I felt my knees buckle. She smelled so good. Her skin was so sexy, and chocolate. Far from the pale skin of my wife that I'd grown so tired of. Even the tanning couldn't get her complexion close enough to satisfy my urges for a black woman. But here was Michelle standing before me in all her African American glory. I wanted to bow down and kiss her perfect toes.

"I-I-I- just thought that you've been doing such a good job. We need more tough Litigants like you. I've watched you in the courtroom and you're—"

"Cut the bullshit, Hupy. You want a piece of this black pussy, don't you? You want to own me. To lay me down and have me do all the things you fantasize about behind your wife's back. You see me in this tight skirt. The way it forms to this rounded ass, and you're dying to know what it looks and feels like when I am naked." She turned around and placed her big booty in my lap, grinding it from side to side over my erection.

I almost fainted, her ass was so nice and soft. It smushed my dick. Then she bent her knees and slowly popped her hips stroking my manhood up and down. I placed my hand on the small of her back. Her booty popped again and again. I felt like she was holding my dick in her fist.

"Admit it, Hupy. This is what you want isn't it, baby?" She stood and hiked her skirt above her waist. Shimmying from right to left until it was where she wanted it to be. Then she turned back around and bent over my desk. A pink thong separated the cheeks. I could see her camel toe from the back. "Well, take it out, white boy. Let me see what you're working with. Hurry up before we're disturbed." She looked over her shoulder at me and smacked her ass.

I fidgeted with my belt until it was undone. Then I pulled out my cock, stroking it furiously from just the sight of all that black skin being out in the open. How could any man not go crazy from those women? I felt like I was losing my mind.

I rushed to her and laid my penis on the crack of her ass. As soon as I did, I came all over it. "Uh-uh!" My knees buckled, and I fell with my face against her wonderful globes.

Before I could even think about standing up, I separated them and started licking in a frenzy. I wanted to taste her rosebud. I Needed to worship this perfect creature. I moaned as I rammed her back door. My chin rubbed against the crotch band that concealed her pussy lips. I licked at it and sucked the lips through the cloth, tasting her sweet juices.

She spread her legs, reached behind her and blocked me from licking her any further. "Hupy, you said the job pays two hundred and fifty thousand dollars a year. Am I correct?" She breathed heavily.

I didn't want to talk about work at this point. I needed to taste her. I needed to get her on my tongue. I could already feel my penis hardening below me. "Michelle, please. I don't want to talk about work, right now. I want to taste this black pussy. I need too! I've waited my whole life for this moment."

She turned all the way around and grabbed me by the throat. "Answer me, white boy! Does it pay two-hundred and fifty thousand dollars a year or not?" She tightened her grip.

I was already stroking my penis. To feel her choking me had me on the verge of cumming all over the floor. This black woman. This Goddess was treating me like I was nothing more than filth, that thought drove me crazy. I needed her so bad. Now I understood the relationship between Trump and Omarosa. Every white man of power needed a black woman to take him down a few pegs.

"Yes-yes! It pays exactly that—" I choked, stroking my cock back and forth at full speed, I needed to cum so bad.

She grabbed my hand away from it and held my wrists. "Now for me. You're going to pay me two hundred and fifty thousand just for allowing you to touch me. I will get three hundred thousand dollars a year for the Senior Partner gig. Do you understand me? That plus all the other perks. Agree to this and I'll surrender this black pussy to you. What do you say, baby?" She held my face in her soft hands, looking into my eyes.

I could smell a hint of her pussy from my position on my knees. I started to shake, I needed this body. I nodded. "Okay, you got it, Michelle, it's yours! Now please let me taste you-please!"

She bent over my desk with that round ass in the air, grabbed my laptop and started to play around it. I didn't know what she was doing, but I was whacking off. Every time she moved in the slightest, her ass would jiggle. That started to drive me crazy. I could see a hint of her pussy lips. I imagined myself sliding into her cave, and nearly came all over my fist again. Finally, she stopped typing and looked over at me with the laptop in her hand.

"All you have to do is complete this transaction. It's for five hundred and fifty thousand. Wire it into this account, and you can have some of this." She took a step back and pulled her panties all the way to the side, exposing her freshly, shaven chocolate garden of bliss. The lips were fully engorged, and looked so pretty, glistening with her juices. Her throbbing clit peered from under its hood, tempting me. I walked closer towards the laptop, in her direction. I clicked send right away, and the transaction went on its way to being completed.

Michelle turned toward me with her legs spread wide. "Eat me, Mr. Hupy. Taste your Nubian, Queen. Own me!"

Without hesitating, I dove my head between her juicy thighs, brushing my nose across her pussy, inhaling her intoxicating scent. I separated her lips and drove my tongue into her hot, moist center, licking it up and down. I drank the nectar that spilled out of her. It tasted sweet with a hint of saltiness. The perfect blend just like I knew it would be. I didn't stop my assault on her pussy until she came all over my mouth and pushed me away from her. I fell onto my back with my dick sticking straight up in the air.

She squatted down and got on all fours with her back to me. "Watch this ass, baby. This the move that made our daddy go crazy." She laid her face on the carpet, and the next thing I knew her ass popped up and down, first the left cheek, then the right. "Come on, baby hit it from the back. Hit this shit! Own me!"

Every time she said the words, "Own Me." It made me want to lose my mind. I wasn't a racist by far, but I swear I understood why so many white men had black women slaves back in the day.

I don't think I would have had any slaves, but then when I imagined having a house full of black women forced to do everything I commanded them to do, I was almost certain I would have. That would have been too hard to pass up. Especially with their dark black skins, and big booties. I would have been in heaven. When I got to her, I kissed her naked ass and pulled her thong down her booty to her upper thighs that were so juicy, I couldn't help biting them. She was built like a hundred-meter Olympic track star, thick and healthy. I got behind her, stroked my penis, and ran it up and down her cave. It was so hot that before I could get inside, I came again, spurting on her backside.

She moaned and opened her knees wider, exposing that pinkness inside of her dark brown pussy lips. "Come on, baby! What are you waiting on?" she groaned.

I squeezed her big booty, then opened it, and played around with the anus. My middle finger slipped into it. It was so tight my second knuckle could barely fit into it.

"That's what you want, baby? Come on then. You've paid for it. If you want some of that big black booty, then hurry up before somebody bothers us." She laid her face on the carpet again and held her cheeks apart for me.

This caused her pussy to open slightly. A trickle of juice seeped out of it and ran down her thigh. Before it could drip to the floor, I licked it and sucked her cunt into my mouth. Then ran my nose up and down its crease. She smelled like a blessing. One I'd never known.

"Uh! Come on, Hupy. Put it in one of those holes-hurry up," She moaned then slid her hand under her belly, into her vagina, tweaking her clit.

I kneeled behind her and once again placed my head directly at the opening of her pussy and pushed forward expecting to cum right away, but luckily for me, I didn't. She slammed back into my lap, impaling herself on me. Then she was twerking that big booty while I held her hips. I sat with my back against the wall while she did her thing to me. Her ass jiggled and shook. My pink penis was devoured by her tight twat.

She got on her elbows looking back at me, with sweat on her forehead. "Watch it, Hupy. Watch it, aww fuck, look at that black ass!"

I shivered and started matching her stroke for stroke. Her pussy was so good. The best I'd ever had in my entire life. I still couldn't believe I was actually inside of her. A Black woman, a Goddess. I felt like nothing else mattered in all the world to me. I was pounding so hard I pulled back too far, and my dick fell out of her. I nearly came again then she picked him up, and put me back inside of her, before slamming into my lap again and again. My phone started to ring, I didn't even care. Somebody started knocking on my office door. I felt her walls sucking at me. I squeezed her cheeks, saw how my cock looked slicing between her brown lips, and it became too much. I smacked her ass as hard as I could and came for the third time deep in her womb while she twerked in my lap. She leaned all the way forward and disconnected us.

She turned around and took a hold of my cock, kissing the sensitive head. "How do you feel, baby? Tell me, I want to know." She slobbered all over my manhood, then took me into her mouth, taking it to the back of her throat. Her back was arched, and her big booty was in the air. I could see that her pussy was bussed wide open from the reflection in my office mirror. The sight caused my dick to harden for the fourth lime.

"I feel like anything you say goes. Anything, I don't care. From here on out. I swear to God above."

She popped me out of her mouth and allowed my penis to rest against her cheek. "We gon' have some fun, baby. Just as long as you know that fun don't come cheap. You hear me?" She licked up my stalk and kissed the head again.

I nodded. "I hear you, and I understand. The promotion is yours!"

It's been three years and I haven't gotten tired of Michelle yet. I wound up making the best decision for the firm by making her a Senior Partner. She's taken our firm to the next level, now it is more integrated and diverse. All I can say is that the power of a black woman is amazing.

Materialistic

About a year ago, I made one of the biggest mistakes of my life when I began sleeping with my best friend's husband. My best friend Kendall, and I have been close since the eleventh grade. Throughout the years she'd become more like a sister to me. Anytime I needed somebody to talk to, or lean on for support, Kendall was there.

About two years ago, I'd been through a very rough break up with a man I was engaged to for three years. It was very hard for me, and I didn't have anybody to lean on, but once again, Kendall stepped up to the plate and was there for me emotionally, as best as she could be. Had she not been there I don't know what I would have done. It was Kendall who convinced me to move here to Houston, Texas, from New Orleans, Louisiana after I'd broken up with my Fiancée. Things were very hard for me at that time, and I desperately needed a new start because everywhere I went in New Orleans, reminded me of my ex-fiancée.

Emotionally, I was unable to handle it. I needed to get out of there, and Kendall said she would be more than happy to put up with me for a few months until I was able to get back on to my feet. At that time, I was a struggling college student, and I was juggling various jobs to make ends meet. So, the only obstacle I saw up ahead was transferring colleges and finding employment in the new city. But I knew I needed to get out of New Orleans, so I packed my things, and two weeks later I was pulling into Kendall's driveway, with a Dodge Durango full of boxes.

Kendall ran out of the house in her small daisy dukes that showed off her thick golden thighs. She also had on a cut off belly shirt that allowed the world to see the diamond in her belly button. Her abs looked like she did crunches all day long.

Her pretty face and long curly hair made her look like she was a model. Even though, I'd never gotten down with any females I could admit my best friend was a Dime in every sense of the word. She'd been the head cheerleader in our school, and before she and I had gotten cool we were at each other's throats and in competition for the crown of the baddest Bitch in our school. She was bad, but I'm not short stopping either.

I am five-feet-seven-inches tall, weigh one-hundred and thirty pounds. Most of my weight is in my ass and thighs. I have light brown eyes, dark brown skin, and a short curly hair tapered on the sides. I make sure I keep myself well-groomed and above standard. I've always been that way, even back in high school when Kendall and I were rivals. Well until the eleventh grade that is. That's the grade where we sort of became too mature for high school and were more focused on boys, and what they could do for us. So, this day, Kendall ran out of the house and hugged me tightly in the driveway.

She was a few inches shorter than me. "Girl, it's about time you got here. I thought you changed your mind or something," She said taking a step back to look at me.

"Never that, I had to get out of that city. Everything was reminding me of Mylo. I'm ready for a fresh start. Thank you for taking me in. I swear, I won't be here that long." I was already feeling like a burden.

I was used to being on my own. I didn't know how I was going to feel once I actually unpacked, and the realization came crashing down that I was actually staying with somebody else.

Kendall wrapped her arms around my shoulder. "Cantrell, you're my sister. This is what sisters do for each other. Girl, I know if I ever broke up with Tim you would do the same for me."

"In a heartbeat." That was all I was able to whisper. I felt my eyes tearing up, I was feeling emotional already. The sun was shining brightly upon us. It felt like it was a hundred plus degrees outside. I was sweating a tad, and ready to get the boxes inside of the house, so I could be under the air conditioner that I was praying she had.

I looked back at my truck. "It's like fifty boxes in there, and the rest I'm having shipped to me. Do we have any help, or—" I smiled but was very serious.

She laughed. "Aw, yeah, you know I ain't about to break a nail. I'm 'bout to make Tim ass move all that shit. He just got back from training camp yesterday. Would you believe he turned down a five-year sixty-million-dollar deal to play with the Los Angeles Lakers, all because he wants to stay here in Houston, so he can be close to his mother?" She shook her head.

"Wow, that's a lot of money. I don't think I could ever turn down that much dough. He must really love his mother."

"Yeah, well, I really love Gucci, and I needed shit. The Rockets gave him fifty million, but the other ten we left on the table. He says he'll make it back through endorsement deals, but that could take forever." She rolled her eyes. "I guess, either way, I'm gon' live the lifestyle

I deserve, so his ass better get a move on cause, I got things I need. Come on girl." She hooked her arm in mine, and we headed into the three-story red bricked home.

It was so beautiful that I instantly became jealous. We found Tim standing in the massive living room watching ESPN's Sports Center. He was tall, standing at six-foot-six. I couldn't tell you how much he weighed, but what I can tell you is that his body was well defined. He had muscles up and down his stomach. His chest puffed out, his nipples were dark brown. He had low cut waves that rippled along the top of his head and tattoos everywhere. My eyes trailed lower to the sweatpants he wore, and I was able to make out his print. It looked to be at least seven inches.

My mouth watered, and when I realized I was lusting after my best friend's husband, I picked up my jaw and snapped out of it.

"Tim, this is, Cantrell. You know my best friend, the one I was telling you about? She's going to be staying here for a little while, so you better treat her as good as you do me. That's an order," Kendall said.

Tim set the remote controller on the glass table and walked over to me with his right hand extended. "It's a pleasure to meet you, Cantrell." He peered into my eyes with his gray ones, and I nearly melted. I knew right then and there that my stay was not going to be an easy one.

* * *

Later that night, Kendall, came into my bedroom with a big smile on her face. "Girl, I already know you are, and you won't accept any money or handouts from me, but you need money while you're getting back on your feet. I can get you a gig at my Uncle's gentlemen's club uptown. The men that come in there are mostly ballers. I'm talking NFL, NBA, MLB, men of that caliber. As good as you dance, I can see you making no less than five thousand a night. That's if you're up to something like that. I mean you don't have to, but I'd cut you a check for fifty thousand, right now if you'd accept it."

I was laid back on the bed reading a book called, *'Loyal to the Game' by T.J. & Jelissa.* It had me so gone it took me a few moments to snap out of the zone. "Wait, say all that again."

She repeated it all and crossed her arms in front of her. "So, what do you think? You down to get money like that or should I just wire you some?" She sat beside me and rested her hand on my thigh.

I had on some comfortable booty shorts and a small tank top. I called it my reading attire. What Kendall didn't know was that I'd stripped at a few clubs back in New Orleans to make ends meet, so it wasn't like the scene was unfamiliar to me. What did sound unfamiliar was the amount of cash she was saying I could walk away with. If I could walk away with a guaranteed five thousand a night, it wouldn't take me much time for me to be back on my feet and into my own place. There was no way I could turn down that opportunity.

I nodded. "That sounds awesome. When would I be able to start?"

She rubbed my thigh and squeezed it in her small hand. "Well, my uncle said he'll have an opening in about two weeks. I guess one of his girls has finally paid her way through Law school. So, you'll be taking her spot. You're gonna be an upgrade I'll tell you that." She sucked her bottom lip into her mouth and continued to stroke my thigh. Her hand moved further and further upward, until her fingers slipped under the band of my booty shorts, poking at my sex lips. "Uh, Kendall, what are you doing?" I asked looking at her fingers.

I was starting to feel some type of way. I don't know why I was, because I had never done anything with a female before.

She pulled my right thigh closer to her, causing me to open my legs wide. "Oh, nothing, I just can't believe how thick you've gotten. I wanna see if your lil' cat is fat, too. Dang, we're both girls, it ain't nothing weird about this. Relax." She rubbed the front of my shorts until a wet spot appeared in the middle of them. Then she pulled them all the way up creating a wedgie with my pussy lips.

"Uh!" I arched my back and opened my legs further. "Kendall, you got me feeling some type of way. You better stop before it goes too far. You're my best friend," I whispered.

She snickered and put her face between my legs. Then kissed my exposed lips, before licking both. "Damn, your lips are fat. Yeah, they gon' love this body. Just wait, you gon' be rolling in the dough." She kissed them each once more, then pulled my shorts back over them.

Before I could say something to her, I noticed Tim was standing in the doorway with bucked eyes and a hard-on in his shorts. He grabbed it and squeezed his pipe. "Baby, come on, I need you, right now," He said holding his left hand out for her. Kendall looked over her shoulder and smiled at him. She stood up with her panties inside her big booty. I mean her globes swallowed them. "I'll holler at you in the morning, Cantrell. Sleep well." She left out of the room and closed the door. As soon as it was closed, I jumped out of the bed and locked it. Then ran back and laid on top of my covers bringing myself to one orgasm after the next imagining what her lips felt like on my kitty.

* * *

I awoke and headed to the kitchen the next morning for breakfast only to find, Kendall at the stove making French toast in just a short tank top that fell to the bottom of her waist, and no panties. Her golden ass cheeks jiggled as she moved back and forth from the stove to the table cooking away. She was singing along to the SZA 'Broken Clocks' song coming out of the speakers. I watched in awe from the hallway afraid to go into the kitchen, not knowing if I would have been impeding on her privacy, or what. I was thinking maybe she was used to getting up and cooking breakfast in such a state. So, instead of breaking her out of her groove, I figured I'd grab my things and take a shower first.

I gathered my things and headed into the bathroom. The way the speakers were set up all around the house. I was able to hear the same music that she was listening to in the kitchen. So, I was jamming to SZA as I showered away, feeling good. I was thankful that I already had a nice paying job lined up for me. My credits had been transferred to the University of Houston. I had a roof over my head for the time being. I was just thankful to, Kendall. I heard the bathroom door open, and close.

That shocked me, I pulled back the curtain to find, Kendall, sliding her tank top over her head.

Her C cup breasts shook on her chest before she stepped into the shower smiling at me. "Dang, Cantrell, you look like you've seen a ghost or something." She took the loofah out of my hand and squirted body wash on to it. She lathered it up and ran it over her body.

I laughed nervously. "It's okay, I was done anyway. I didn't mean to be in here so long." I started to get out when she grabbed my hand.

"Un-uh. You ain't going nowhere I want you to shower with me. I can use the extra help." She stepped into my face backing me up against the wall in the shower. "Besides, I was bogus for leaving you like that last night." Her hand rubbed down my stomach, and in between my legs. Her finger slipped between my bald lips, opening me. She sucked on my neck. "I've wanted to do this to you for so long." Two of her fingers entered me.

I bucked against her hand and started shaking. "Kendall, your fingers are in me. You're fingering me. What's the matter with you?" I moaned and set my foot on the rim of the tub giving her all the access she needed. I held onto her shoulders. Her fingers ran in and out of me at full speed.

Her thumb ran circles around my clitoris bringing me closer and closer to my ending. "Cum for me, Cantrell. Cum for me. It's good, I know this fat pussy wanna cum." She bit into my neck and grabbed my right breast.

That was all it took, I screamed out loud and came all over her stabbing fingers. After I came, she pulled them out of me and sucked them into her mouth. "Damn, you taste good. I'm glad you're here girl."

* * *

Although the money was as good as promised, the men at the club were head cases. All of them were overly conceited and felt like a girl should go above and beyond for them just because they were professional athletes. I didn't give a care what they were, or what they thought. I got away with doing as little as I possibly could, so I could get on to the next patron. I was always joyful when the end of my shift came. I'd sit in the dressing room and count my money, give Kendall's uncle his cut, and be out. Then get back home, and to sleep before getting ready to do more of the same, the next day. Kendall continued to flirt with me every single day. She made it her business to corner me in certain places in the house, so she could feel all over my body, or go down on me.

For some reason, she was obsessed with my taste. I didn't mind her doing the things she did to me because they felt so good. I was just curious as to where all her sexual feelings toward me had come from. All she said was that she'd been feeling them ever since we were in the ninth grade. We were enemies at that time, so I didn't get it, but I didn't ask her to explain either.

About a month after I moved to Houston, Tim, started bringing me bags and bags of expensive gifts and clothes every time he'd bring some for, Kendall. In a matter of two months, he turned my whole closet into nothing but high-end designer clothes, purses, bags, and shoes. I didn't have to spend any of the money I made at the club on anything like that, and I was so grateful. I always offered to pay him for them, but he'd decline my offers with a big dimpled smile.

In addition to all the expensive things he bought me, I noticed him watching me a lot as I walked around the house or sat talking to Kendall. Whenever I'd look over at him, he'd divert his eyes and blush. That always made me laugh. I guess I could tell he was feeling me in such a way. I didn't know how to feel about that because I knew I would never betray Kendall. I loved her with all my heart.

* * *

Then, one day I was summoned to the floor of the club. The second-floor Private room of the club was re-served strictly for supreme ballers. It cost ten thousand dollars just to book a room. Then another five thousand to have the bar rented for the whole night. That was fif-teen thousand. Upon paying that amount the patron could take his pick to have any four strippers of his choosing for the entire night. He would be supplied un-limited table and lap dances in the privacy of the room. Where there was no cameras allowed, no phones, and no bouncers.

Each stripper that catered to one of these V.I.P. gen-tlemen were paid a stipend of five thousand dollars up front, not including tips. I wasn't called up to the private room until I was literally two hours away from my shift ending for the night. This day the club was kind of slow, I'd only made two thousand to take home, so to be called upstairs was sort of bittersweet for me. It was bitter be-cause I didn't know how long this private session would last, and what the patron would request. Some were too demanding and refused to stick to the no touching policy.

Had I gotten one of them I would have to forfeit the money, I'd done that twice before. But it was sweet because I knew I would be walking out of the doors that night with no less than seven-grand. That was the good part. As long as the Patron was respectful and stuck to the rules. I'd give him or her any dance they wanted. But, imagine my face when I knocked on the door, and it opened to reveal Tim with two big bundles of cash in his hands. My jaw dropped, I felt like I couldn't breathe.

"Shawty, before you say anything all I want is a few dances. I been peeping you ever since you got over here from New Orleans. I think you bad Ma'. I know my shawty been going in on you because every time she come out of your room, I can taste your pussy on her tongue. I don't think, I've ever tongued her down more than I have been doing since you've been here. I got a thing for you. Come on in." He grabbed my hand and pulled me inside, closing the door.

"Tim, I don't know what to say. I mean, what would Kendall say if she knew you were here, right now? She'd probably kill you."

He held up the two big stacks of cash. "Shawty, I don't care. This twenty-gees right here, and it's all yours. I'm trying to cash you out. I'll buy you a whole ass house, and a new truck. It's whatever you like. Money ain't an object, just name your price?" He handed me the first stack of cash they were big faced hundreds.

I took it and set it on the table that was filled with more money, bottles of Moet, and Cîroc. I could tell he'd come to party. He came from behind me and rubbed my exposed booty.

"You see what I'm talking about. You're so strapped, Shawty. They ain't got ass like this down here in, Houston, not real ones. You gon' have to let me get some of this one way or the other." His hand slipped between my crease and rubbed my pussy through the material.

I closed my eyes as I imagined Kendall's sexy face. Then I imagined it angry, and that scared me. I stood up and pushed him away from me. "I can't do this, Tim. I love Kendall way too much. She's my girl, you know?"

He shook his head and tossed the bundle of cash into the air so that it rained down all around us. "I love her, too, but I gotta have me some of you. I'll deal with the consequences later. Get yo' fine ass over here." He grabbed me into his embrace, pressing his forehead against mine.

His big hands cupped my booty that was encased in red lace boy shorts, that was way too small for me. I was naked underneath them. I held a hand against his chest trying with as much strength as I could muster to push him off me. "Tim, let me go. I'm not gon' betray my friend like this. I just can't."

"Shawty, I'll take care of you. She ain't gotta know nothing. I see how your face lights up every time I drop them Gucci bags in front of you. That ain't shit, all you gotta do is fuck wit' me and I'll make that a habit. A woman as fine as you shouldn't have no worries. Not when it's men like me around." He rubbed my ass and covered my lips with his own.

They were soft, yet firm. I found myself sinking into the abyss of him. But once again, Kendall's face popped into my mind. I struggled to push him away. "Get off me, Tim. All that stuff sound good, but I ain't goin'." I twisted my body as hard as I could, then pushed myself out of his grasp, falling on the couch.

He dropped to his knees and pried my thighs apart. "At least let me taste you like she did. Let me see what this honey taste like right from the source." He yanked my boy shorts to the side and ran his tongue up and down my crease. He slurped my pussy into his mouth. "Mmm, shit," He groaned pushing my knees to my chest. The sounds he made got louder and louder the more he got into the act.

I closed my eyes, trapped. I couldn't move from the waist down. His tongue felt like it was eight inches long. It explored every nook and cranny of my pussy and ass. By the time he finished with me, I'd cum three times, and he was still eating me.

I bucked on the couch and screamed. "Aw, Tim, I can't take no more. I can't take no more, baby, please!" My clit was so sensitive even the air in the room was sending tingles through me. It stood out at the top of my sex lips erect and throbbing. Tim stood and pulled his dick out of his pants. It looked like it had to be at least ten inches long. It was thick and full of veins. The head looked like the Arby's symbol.

He straddled my waist and rubbed it against my lips. "Come on, Cantrell. Come on, baby. Handle this bidness for me." I was so horny and wet by this point all caution was thrown to the wind.

I couldn't wait to get him inside my mouth, and just being honest, I had been thinking that way ever since I stepped foot in their home. I took a hold of his big dick, licked the head, then sucked him into my mouth, spearing my head into his lap taking as much of him as I possibly could.

His eyes rolled backward, he humped into my lips, grabbing my curly hair. "Ugh-ugh-ugh, Cantrell! Damn, you so fucking bad, Ma. Fuck this." He pulled out of my mouth.

His dick throbbed against his stomach. If it hadn't been eleven inches before now it looked like it had grown a few more inches. He pulled me up and bent me over the couch, yanking my panties all the way down my thighs, rubbing in between them. "I gotta hit this shit. It's twenty thousand on this floor. All of it is yours. I'll holla at my Realtor tomorrow, too. We gon' put you in your own shit. Just let me hit this pussy, and we keep this night on the down low. Don't worry, I'ma take care of you girl." He smacked my ass and kicked my legs apart.

I held the back of the couch. I felt his big dick opening my lips, then in one lunge, he was buried halfway inside my pussy. I came instantly, falling face first into the couch. He pulled me back up and fucked me like a maniac. His long dick sawed in and out of my pussy, while his finger played with my asshole.

"Uh-uh, shit-shit, Cantrell! Cantrell, you got that muthafuckin' snapper-shit!" He was going so hard and fast, I couldn't keep up.

"Tim, oh un, Tim. What about-what about, Kendall. Aw shit!" I screamed as another orgasm coursed through me. I started to shake, coating his dick with my juice.

He pulled out, picked me up and slammed me to the couch. Then pushed my knees to my breasts and really put a-hurtin' on my shit. I could feel him in my fucking stomach. I came again, and again. I passed out and woke up to him still going hard. I closed my eyes as another orgasm ripped through me. I didn't know how much more I could take.

"Cantrell, I'm about to cum, Shawty. I'm 'bout to cum in this tight ass pussy. Aw fuck, Shawty-shit!" He hollered and speeded his pace long stroking me like a Monster.

I was screaming and cumming all over his dick, it felt so good. I loved Kendall, but his dick was so good. I mean, I can't even explain now as I write this. But the harder he fucked me, the harder I came until I passed out. I don't know how long I was gone, but when my eyes finally opened, not only was Tim standing over me but beside him stood Kendall.

She had her arm wrapped around his lower waist, smiling down on me. "Bitch, I knew you couldn't be trusted around my nigga. Look at you." She threw a bundle of money in my face. Took the bottle of Moet and sipped from it. "What you think, Honey? You think she bad enough to add to this threesome?" She questioned Tim.

He shook his head. "Naw, this bitch can't be trusted. Any woman that'll fuck her best friend's husband, after all you did for her, can't be trusted." he kissed his teeth. "That's a shame, though."

Kendall took the bottle of Moet and poured it all over me. "Here you go, bitch. That's what you get for being thirsty."

Crazy thing about this story, is that it didn't end there. You see, Tim might've been spitting all that bullshit in front of Kendall, but not only did I wind up pregnant from this night, but before I pushed out his twins, Tim and I walked down the aisle. We've been married going four months now. Kendall decided to step to the side and go her separate ways after a hefty divorce settlement.

Yea, I'm a bogus bitch but what can I say, shit happens!

Submission Guideline

Submit the first three chapters of your completed manuscript to ldpsubmissions@gmail.com, subject line: Your book's title. The manuscript must be in a .doc file and sent as an attachment. Document should be in Times New Roman, double spaced and in size 12 font. Also, provide your synopsis and full contact information. If sending multiple submissions, they must each be in a separate email.

Have a story but no way to send it electronically? You can still submit to LDP/Ca$h Presents. Send in the first three chapters, written or typed, of your completed manuscript to:

LDP: Submissions Dept
Po Box 870494
Mesquite, Tx 75187

DO NOT send original manuscript. Must be a duplicate.

Provide your synopsis and a cover letter containing your full contact information.

Thanks for considering LDP and Ca$h Presents.

<u>Coming Soon from Lock Down Publications/Ca$h Presents</u>

BOW DOWN TO MY GANGSTA

By **Ca$h**

TORN BETWEEN TWO

By **Coffee**

BLOOD STAINS OF A SHOTTA **III**

By **Jamaica**

STEADY MOBBIN **III**

By **Marcellus Allen**

BLOOD OF A BOSS **V**

By **Askari**

LOYAL TO THE GAME **IV**

LIFE OF SIN

By **T.J. & Jelissa**

A DOPEBOY'S PRAYER **II**

By **Eddie "Wolf" Lee**

IF LOVING YOU IS WRONG… **III**

LOVE ME EVEN WHEN IT HURTS **II**

By **Jelissa**

TRUE SAVAGE **VI**

By **Chris Green**

BLAST FOR ME **III**

A BRONX TALE

By **Ghost**

ADDICTIED TO THE DRAMA **III**

Cum For Me 4

By **Jamila Mathis**
LIPSTICK KILLAH **III**
CRIME OF PASSION **II**
By **Mimi**
WHAT BAD BITCHES DO **III**
KILL ZONE **II**
By **Aryanna**
THE COST OF LOYALTY **II**
By **Kweli**
SHE FELL IN LOVE WITH A REAL ONE **II**
By **Tamara Butler**
LOVE SHOULDN'T HURT **III**
RENEGADE BOYS **II**
By **Meesha**
CORRUPTED BY A GANGSTA **III**
By **Destiny Skai**
A GANGSTER'S CODE **III**
By **J-Blunt**
KING OF NEW YORK III
By **T.J. Edwards**
CUM FOR ME **IV**
By **Ca$h & Company**
GORILLAS IN THE BAY
De'Kari
THE STREETS ARE CALLING
Duquie Wilson
KINGPIN KILLAZ II

Hood Rich
STEADY MOBBIN' **III**
Marcellus Allen
SINS OF A HUSTLER
ASAD
HER MAN, MINE'S TOO **II**
Nicole Goosby
GORILLAZ IN THE BAY **II**
DE'KARI
KINGZ OF THE GAME
Playa Ray

Available Now
RESTRAINING ORDER **I & II**
By **CA$H & Coffee**
LOVE KNOWS NO BOUNDARIES **I II & III**
By **Coffee**
RAISED AS A GOON I, II, III & IV
BRED BY THE SLUMS I, II, III
BLAST FOR ME I & II
ROTTEN TO THE CORE I III
By **Ghost**
LAY IT DOWN **I & II**
LAST OF A DYING BREED
BLOOD STAINS OF A SHOTTA I & II
By **Jamaica**

LOYAL TO THE GAME
LOYAL TO THE GAME II
LOYAL TO THE GAME III
By **TJ & Jelissa**
BLOODY COMMAS I & II
SKI MASK CARTEL I II & III
KING OF NEW YORK I II
By **T.J. Edwards**
IF LOVING HIM IS WRONG…I & II
LOVE ME EVEN WHEN IT HURTS
By **Jelissa**
WHEN THE STREETS CLAP BACK I & II III
By **Jibril Williams**
A DISTINGUISHED THUG STOLE MY HEART I II & III
LOVE SHOULDN'T HURT I II
RENEGADE BOYS
By **Meesha**
A GANGSTER'S CODE I & II
By **J-Blunt**
PUSH IT TO THE LIMIT
By **Bre' Hayes**
BLOOD OF A BOSS **I, II, III & IV**
By **Askari**
THE STREETS BLEED MURDER **I, II & III**
THE HEART OF A GANGSTA I II& III
By **Jerry Jackson**
CUM FOR ME

Ca$h & Company

CUM FOR ME 2

CUM FOR ME 3

An **LDP Erotica Collaboration**

BRIDE OF A HUSTLA **I II & II**

THE FETTI GIRLS **I, II& III**

CORRUPTED BY A GANGSTA I & II

By **Destiny Skai**

WHEN A GOOD GIRL GOES BAD

By **Adrienne**

A GANGSTER'S REVENGE **I II III & IV**

THE BOSS MAN'S DAUGHTERS

THE BOSS MAN'S DAUGHTERS II

THE BOSSMAN'S DAUGHTERS III

THE BOSSMAN'S DAUGHTERS IV

THE BOSS MAN'S DAUGHTERS **V**

A SAVAGE LOVE **I & II**

BAE BELONGS TO ME

A HUSTLER'S DECEIT I, II

WHAT BAD BITCHES DO I, II

By **Aryanna**

A KINGPIN'S AMBITON

A KINGPIN'S AMBITION **II**

I MURDER FOR THE DOUGH

By **Ambitious**

TRUE SAVAGE

TRUE SAVAGE II

TRUE SAVAGE **III**

TRUE SAVAGE **IV**

TRUE SAVAGE **V**

By **Chris Green**

A DOPEBOY'S PRAYER

By **Eddie "Wolf" Lee**

THE KING CARTEL **I, II & III**

By **Frank Gresham**

THESE NIGGAS AIN'T LOYAL **I, II & III**

By **Nikki Tee**

GANGSTA SHYT **I II &III**

By **CATO**

THE ULTIMATE BETRAYAL

By **Phoenix**

BOSS'N UP **I , II & III**

By **Royal Nicole**

I LOVE YOU TO DEATH

By Destiny J

I RIDE FOR MY HITTA

I STILL RIDE FOR MY HITTA

By **Misty Holt**

LOVE & CHASIN' PAPER

By **Qay Crockett**

TO DIE IN VAIN

By **ASAD**

BROOKLYN HUSTLAZ

By **Boogsy Morina**

BROOKLYN ON LOCK I & II

Ca$h & Company

By **Sonovia**

GANGSTA CITY

By **Teddy Duke**

A DRUG KING AND HIS DIAMOND I & II III

A DOPEMAN'S RICHES

HER MAN, MINE'S TOO

By Nicole Goosby

TRAPHOUSE KING **I II & III**

KINGPIN KILLAZ

By **Hood Rich**

LIPSTICK KILLAH **I, II**

CRIME OF PASSION

By **Mimi**

STEADY MOBBN' **I, II**

By **Marcellus Allen**

WHO SHOT YA **I, II**

Renta

GORILLAZ IN THE BAY

DE'KARI

BOOKS BY LDP'S CEO, CA$H

TRUST IN NO MAN

TRUST IN NO MAN 2

TRUST IN NO MAN 3

BONDED BY BLOOD

SHORTY GOT A THUG

THUGS CRY

THUGS CRY 2

THUGS CRY 3

TRUST NO BITCH

TRUST NO BITCH 2

TRUST NO BITCH 3

TIL MY CASKET DROPS

RESTRAINING ORDER

RESTRAINING ORDER 2

IN LOVE WITH A CONVICT

Coming Soon

BONDED BY BLOOD 2

BOW DOWN TO MY GANGSTA

Ca$h & Company

www.ingramcontent.com/pod-product-compliance
Lightning Source LLC
Chambersburg PA
CBHW051225260626
47161CB00005BA/1693